FYODOR
DOSTOYEVSKY

Notes from Underground

Translated by RONALD WILKS

PENGUIN BOOKS

PENGUIN CLASSICS

Published by the Penguin Group
Penguin Books Ltd, 80 Strand, London WC2R 0RL, England
Penguin Group (USA) Inc., 375 Hudson Street, New York, New York 10014, USA
Penguin Group (Canada), 90 Eglinton Avenue East, Suite 700, Toronto, Ontario, Canada M4P 2Y3
(a division of Pearson Penguin Canada Inc.)
Penguin Ireland, 25 St Stephen's Green, Dublin 2, Ireland (a division of Penguin Books Ltd)
Penguin Group (Australia), 250 Camberwell Road, Camberwell, Victoria 3124, Australia
(a division of Pearson Australia Group Pty Ltd)
Penguin Books India Pvt Ltd, 11 Community Centre, Panchsheel Park, New Delhi – 110 017, India
Penguin Group (NZ), 67 Apollo Drive, Rosedale, North Shore 0632, New Zealand
(a division of Pearson New Zealand Ltd)
Penguin Books (South Africa) (Pty) Ltd, 24 Sturdee Avenue, Rosebank, Johannesburg 2196, South Africa

Penguin Books Ltd, Registered Offices: 80 Strand, London WC2R 0RL, England

www.penguin.com

Notes from Underground first published 1864
This translation first published in Penguin Classics 2009
This (PENGUIN CLASSICS) RED edition published 2010
2

Set in 10.25/12.25 pt PostScript Adobe Sabon
Printed in England by Clays Ltd, St Ives plc

ISBN: 978-0-141-19438-7

www.greenpenguin.co.uk

Contents

n a book save lives? This one can.

nguin Classics have inspired the imaginations of millions of aders all over the world, transforming the way people think and l for ever. And now that we've partnered with (PRODUCT)RED™ to bring u our selection of some of the best stories ever written as (PENGUIN CLASSICS)RED editions, books are going to help save lives too.

Penguin will be contributing 50% of our profits from these (PENGUIN CLASSICS)RED editions to the Global Fund to help eliminate AIDS in Africa.

So far, 4 million lives have been reached by the Global Fund-financed programmes supported by (RED)™. These programmes provide antiretroviral drugs, HIV rapid test kits, HIV-related training for medical and counselling staff, and Prevention of Mother to Child Transmission (or PMTCT) treatments. Not one penny is taken out of the Global Fund for overheads, so every single pound goes straight to the people who need help, and straight to keeping them alive so that they can go on taking care of their families, living their lives and changing their own worlds.

Buy a piece of great literature and do something great.

PENGUIN CLASSICS IS A PROUD PARTNER OF (PRODUCT)RED™

I
*The Underground**

I'm a sick man . . . I'm a spiteful man. I'm an unattractive man. I think there's something wrong with my liver. But I understand damn all about my illness and I can't say for certain which part of me is affected. I'm not receiving treatment for it and never have, although I do respect medicine and doctors. What's more, I'm still extremely superstitious – well, sufficiently to respect medicine. (I'm educated enough not to be superstitious, but I am superstitious.) Oh no, I'm refusing treatment out of spite. That's something you probably can't bring yourselves to understand. Well, I understand it. Of course, in this case I can't explain exactly to you whom I'm trying to harm by my spite. I realize perfectly well that I cannot 'besmirch' the doctors by not consulting them. I know better than anyone that by all this I'm harming no one but myself. All the same, if I refuse to have treatment it's out of spite. So, if my liver hurts, let it hurt even more!

I've been living like this for a long time – about twenty years. I'm forty now. I used to work in a government department, but

* The author of these notes and the *Notes* themselves are, of course, fictitious. Nevertheless, such people as the writer of these notes not only can but even must exist in our society – taking into consideration those circumstances in which our society was formed. I wanted to bring before the public more distinctly than usual one of the characters of the recent past. He is a representative of a generation that has survived to this day. In this fragment entitled *The Underground*, this person introduces himself and his views, and apparently wishes to explain those reasons as a result of which that generation appeared and was bound to appear in our midst. In the second fragment there appear the actual notes of this person about certain events in his life.

Fyodor Dostoyevsky

I don't work there any more. I was a spiteful civil servant. I was rude and enjoyed being rude. You see, I never took bribes, so I had to compensate myself in some way. (That's a rotten joke, but I don't intend striking it out. I wrote it down thinking it could come across very witty, but now that I've seen that I only wanted to do a spot of vulgar bragging I shall let it stand on purpose!) Whenever people came with their petitions to the desk where I sat I would snarl at them and I felt inexhaustible pleasure whenever I succeeded in upsetting someone. And I was nearly always successful. For the most part they were a timid bunch – we all know what people asking for favours are like. But among those fops there was one particular officer whom I just couldn't stand. He simply wouldn't be brought to heel and had a nasty way of rattling his sabre. For eighteen months he and I waged war over that sabre. In the end I triumphed. He stopped the rattling. However, this happened when I was still young. And do you know, gentlemen, what was the main point of my malice? Well, the main point, indeed the crowning nastiness, was that even during my most splenetic moments I was constantly, shamefully, aware that not only was I not seething with spite but that I wasn't even embittered, and was merely scaring sparrows in vain, for my own amusement. I might foam at the mouth, but just bring me some kind of toy, give me a cup of tea with sugar and most likely I'd calm down or even be deeply touched, although I'd be so ashamed. I would most certainly grumble at myself afterwards and suffer from insomnia for several months. I've always been like that.

Well, I lied about myself just now when I said I was a spiteful civil servant. I lied out of spite. I was simply having a little fun with these petitioners and the officer, as in fact I could never really be spiteful. I was always conscious of the abundance of elements within me that were diametrically opposed to that. I felt that they were literally swarming inside me, those warring elements. I knew that they had been swarming there all my life, begging to be set free, but I wouldn't set them free, oh no, I wouldn't, I deliberately wouldn't set them free. They tormented me until I felt ashamed; they brought on convulsions and – in the end – they bored me, oh how they bored me! So don't you think, gentlemen, that I'm repenting of something to you, asking you to forgive me for something? I'm certain that's what you think. But I assure you that it's all the same to me if that's what you're thinking . . .

Not only did I not become spiteful, I never even managed to become anything: neither spiteful, nor good, neither a scoundrel nor an honest man, neither a hero nor an insect. And now I'm living out my life in my corner, teasing myself with the spiteful and utterly worthless consolation that an intelligent man cannot make himself anything and that it's only fools who manage to do that. Oh yes, your intelligent, nineteenth-century man ought to be and is in fact morally obliged to be essentially without character; a man of character, a man of action, is primarily a very limited creature. That's my conviction as a forty-year-old. Yes, I'm forty now – mind you, forty is an entire lifetime, it's extreme old age. To go on living after forty is unseemly, vulgar and immoral! Who lives longer than forty? Give me a straight, honest answer. I'll tell you who does: fools and rogues. I shall tell all those venerable old men, all those hoary-haired, sweet-smelling worthies that to their faces! I shall tell the whole world to its face! I have the right to talk like this, since I myself shall live to be sixty. I'll live to be seventy! To be eighty! Now wait a moment! Let me get my breath back . . .

You're probably thinking, gentlemen, that I want to make you laugh. Well, there you're mistaken too. I'm not in the least the jolly type you think I am, or perhaps may think I am. If, however, you find all this chatter irritating (and I can sense that you *are* irritated) and are thinking of asking me who I am exactly, I'd give you this answer: I'm just an ordinary collegiate assessor.[1] I worked in the civil service in order to earn my bread (but solely for that reason) and when a distant relative left me six thousand roubles in his will last year I resigned immediately and settled down in my little corner. I did live for a while in this corner before, but now I've taken up permanent residence in it. My room is cheap and filthy, on the outskirts of town. My maidservant is an old peasant woman, ill-tempered from stupidity, and what's more she always smells terribly. I'm told the St Petersburg climate is bad for me now and that with my paltry means it must be very expensive living in St Petersburg. I know all that, better than all those experienced and extremely wise counsellors and head-shakers. But I shall stay in St Petersburg – I shall not leave St Petersburg! I shan't leave it because . . . Ah well! – it doesn't make a damned bit of difference whether I leave it or not.

However, what can a decent chap talk about with the greatest pleasure?

Answer: about himself.

Very well, I'll talk about myself.

II

Now I'd like to tell you, gentlemen, whether you want to hear it or not, why I didn't even manage to become an insect. I solemnly declare that many times have I wanted to become an insect. But even that hasn't been granted me. I assure you, gentlemen, that to be excessively conscious is a disease, a real, full-blown disease. For the needs of everyday life ordinary human consciousness should be more than sufficient – that is, half or even a quarter less than the portion which falls to the lot of an educated man in our unhappy nineteenth century and, on top of that, of one who has the twofold misfortune of living in St Petersburg, the most abstract and premeditated city on earth. (Cities tend to be either premeditated or unpremeditated.) For example, the consciousness possessed by all our so-called spontaneous people and men of action should be quite sufficient. I'd wager that you think I'm writing all this simply to show off, to score off those men of action and, what's more, that I'm rattling my sabre like my officer, also to show off – and in very bad taste. But gentlemen, who could possibly pride himself on his infirmities, let alone brag about them?

But what am I saying? – everyone does it – everyone vaunts his illnesses – and perhaps myself more than anyone. But don't let us argue about it. I put it rather clumsily. All the same, I'm firmly convinced that not only a great deal of consciousness but even any amount of consciousness is a disease. I firmly maintain that. But let's put that to one side for a moment. Tell me this: why did it invariably happen, as if deliberately, that at those very moments when I was most capable of appreciating all the subtleties of the 'sublime and beautiful'[2] as we once used to say, I not only would fail to comprehend but would perform the most contemptible actions . . . well . . . the kind of which everyone is guilty, but which I happened to perform precisely when I was most conscious that I should not be performing them at all? The more I recognized goodness and the whole question of the 'sublime and beautiful', the deeper I sank into the mire and the more capable I became of completely immersing myself in it. But the main feature of all this was that it wasn't within me by accident, but as if it were bound to be there. It was as if this were my normal condition and far from being an illness or the fruits of corruption, so that finally I lost the desire to combat that corruption. It all ended by my almost coming to believe (or perhaps I really did believe) that this was probably my normal condition. But at the very outset how much agony I was forced to endure in that struggle! I didn't believe the same could happen to others and so all my life I have kept it to myself, like a secret. I was ashamed (and perhaps I'm ashamed now). It reached the point where I felt an abnormal, secret, base thrill of pleasure when returning to my corner on some positively foul St Petersburg night and I would feel intensely aware that once again I had done something vile that day, that what's done cannot be undone, and inwardly, secretly, I would keep gnawing, gnawing, nibbling and eating away at myself until the bitterness finally turned into some shameful, damnable sweetness and finally into serious, definite pleasure. Yes, pleasure, pleasure! I stand by that. I broached the subject because I'd like to find out for certain: do others experience the same kind of pleasure? Let me explain: the pleasure I experienced came directly from being too vividly aware of my own degradation, from the feeling of having gone too far; that it was foul but that it couldn't be otherwise; that there's no way out for you, that you'd never make yourself a different person; that even if there remained enough time and faith to change yourself into something different you most probably wouldn't want to change yourself. And that even if you did want to, you'd end up by doing nothing because there might in fact be nothing to change yourself into. But finally, and most importantly, all this proceeds from the normal, fundamental laws of heightened consciousness and from the inertia which is the direct result of those laws and therefore not only could you *not* change yourself, you'd simply do nothing at all. For instance, as a result of this intensified awareness you are justified in being a scoundrel, as if it's of any comfort to a scoundrel that he himself feels that he's in fact a scoundrel. But that's enough . . . Good Lord, I've been waffling away, and what have I explained? How can one explain this feeling of pleasure? But I shall explain it! I shall pursue it to the bitter end! That's why I picked up my pen . . .

I, for example, am extremely touchy. I'm as suspicious and as quick to take offence as a hunchback or a dwarf, but in fact there have been moments when, if someone had slapped my face, I might have been glad even of that. I mean this in all seriousness: very likely I would have managed to derive pleasure of a kind even from that – I mean of course the pleasure of despair; but it's in despair that you discover the most intense pleasure, especially when you are acutely conscious of the hopelessness of your predicament. And here too, after that slap in the face, you are crushed by the realization of what filth you're being smeared with. The main thing is that, whichever way I look at it, it invariably turns out that I'm the first to be blamed for everything and, what hurts most of all, that I'm blamed when innocent, according to the laws of nature, so to speak. First of all I'm to blame, as I'm cleverer than anyone else around me. (I've always considered myself cleverer than everyone else around me and sometimes, would you believe, even felt ashamed of it. At all events, all my life I've somehow always looked away and could never look people straight in the face.) And finally, I'm guilty, since even if I'd had the magnanimity within me, my awareness of its utter futility would have caused me greater torments. I should probably have been unable to do anything because of my magnanimity: neither forgive, since the offender might have slapped me according to the laws of nature and you can't forgive the laws of nature; nor forget, since even if these are laws of nature it still hurts. Finally, even had I not wanted to be magnanimous at all but, on the contrary, if I'd wanted to take revenge on the offender, most probably I wouldn't even have been able to avenge myself on anyone for anything, since I probably would never have had the determination to do anything even if I could. Why shouldn't I have had the determination? I'd like to say a few words about that in particular.

III

Now, with those people who, for example, know how to take revenge and generally stand up for themselves – how do they do it? They are so obsessed, let's suppose, by this feeling of revenge that during that time all that remains in their entire being is this feeling. This kind of gentleman simply heads straight for his goal like a maddened bull with lowered horns and is stopped only by a wall. (Incidentally, such gentlemen, that's to say, these spontaneous men of action, genuinely give up when faced with a wall. For them a wall is not simply a diversion, as it is, for example, for men like us who think and who consequently do nothing. Nor is it a pretext for turning back, a pretext in which people like us don't normally believe but of which we are always very glad. No, they capitulate in all sincerity. For them a wall provides something reassuring, something morally decisive, definitive, perhaps even something mystical . . . But more about the wall later.) So, it's precisely this kind of spontaneous man whom I consider the real, normal person, such as tender Mother Nature herself wished to see him as she lovingly brought him into being on this earth. This kind of man makes me green with envy. He is stupid – that I don't dispute with you, but perhaps your normal man ought to be stupid – how do you know? Perhaps it's even a very fine thing. And I'm all the more convinced of this suspicion, so to speak, because if one takes for example the antithesis of the normal man, that is, the man of heightened consciousness, who of course has not sprung from the bosom of nature but from a test tube (this is already verging on mysticism, gentlemen, but I'm suspicious of that, too), then this test-tube man will sometimes capitulate when confronted with his antithesis, to such a degree that for all his heightened awareness he will in all good conscience consider himself a mouse and not a man. Granted, an intensely aware mouse, but a mouse all the same, whereas the other is a man, so consequently . . . etc, etc. The important thing is that he, of his own accord, considers himself a mouse: no one asked him to do so – and that's an important point.

But now let's take a look at this mouse in action. Let's suppose, for example, that he too has been offended (and his feelings are almost invariably hurt) and is also thirsting for revenge. Perhaps there is even more anger accumulated in him than in *l'homme de la nature et de la vérité*.[3] That nasty, mean, petty desire to repay the offender in his own coin might possibly gnaw away inside him more viciously than in *l'homme de la nature et de la vérité*, because *l'homme de la nature et de la vérité*, given his inborn stupidity, considers his revenge nothing more than simple, straightforward justice, whereas the mouse, with his heightened awareness, denies there is any justice here. Finally, we come to the deed itself, the act of revenge. In addition to that original nastiness, the hapless mouse has this time managed to accumulate so much additional nastiness in the form of questions and doubts; it has piled up so many other unresolved questions in addition to the original problem that it has involuntarily surrounded itself with a lethal brew, a stinking bog consisting of its doubts and emotions, and finally of the spittle showered on it by all the spontaneous men of action solemnly gathered around in the guise of judges and dictators who are laughing their heads off at him. Of course, it's obvious that all that remains for him to do is wave his little paw dismissively and creep ignominiously back into his little hole with a smile of simulated contempt in which he doesn't even believe himself. There, in his foul, stinking cellar, our offended, downtrodden and ridiculed mouse immerses himself in cold, venomous and, chiefly, everlasting spite. For forty years on end he will remember the offence, down to the smallest and most shameful detail, constantly adding even more shameful details of his own, maliciously teasing and irritating himself with his own fantasies. He himself will be ashamed of his fantasies, but nevertheless he will remember all of them, weighing them up and inventing all sorts of things that never happened to him, on the pretext that they too could have happened and he'll forgive nothing. Probably he'll start taking his revenge, but somehow in fits and starts, pettily, anonymously, from behind the stove, believing neither in his right to take revenge, nor in the success of his revenge and knowing beforehand that he will suffer one hundred times more from every single one of his attempts at revenge than the object of his revenge, who, most likely, won't give a damn. On his deathbed he will recall the whole thing with compound interest for all that time and . . . But it is in this cold, loathsome half-despair, this half-belief, this conscious self-interment in the underground for forty years from sorrow, in that powerfully created but nonetheless partially dubious hopelessness of his situation, in all the poison of inwardly turned, unfulfilled desires, in all those feverish vacillations, in all those decisions taken once and for all only to be regretted a few minutes later, that lies the very essence of that strange pleasure of which I was speaking. It is so subtle and sometimes so little subject to consciousness that even marginally limited people or even strong-nerved people cannot make head or tail of it. Perhaps you will interrupt with a grin – those who have never had their faces slapped won't understand it either – and thus you politely point out to me that at some time in my life I too have perhaps been slapped and that's why I'm speaking as an expert. I'm ready to bet that's what you think. But don't worry, gentlemen, I've never received any slaps, although I'm completely indifferent to what you may think about it. Perhaps I even still regret having distributed so few slaps in my lifetime. But that's enough, not another word on this subject which is so extraordinarily interesting for you.

I shall calmly continue about those people with strong nerves who don't understand certain refinements of pleasure. Although, on different occasions, these gentlemen may roar full-throatedly like bulls and although this supposedly does them the greatest credit, as I've already said, when confronted with an impossibility they immediately capitulate. Impossibility is a stone wall. Now what do I mean by stone wall? Well, the laws of nature, the conclusions of natural science and mathematics of course. Once it is proven to you, for example, that you're descended from the apes,[4] it's no good pulling a long face – you must accept things as they are. Or when they demonstrate that one ounce of your own fat should essentially be dearer to you than a hundred thousand of your fellow men and that this demonstration finally settles the whole question of so-called virtues and duties and other such ravings and prejudices, you must simply accept it, there's nothing you can do about it, since twice two is mathematics. Just you try and refute it.

'If you don't mind!' they'll shout at you, 'you can't fight it: this is twice two is four! Nature doesn't ask for your permission; she's not concerned about your wishes or whether or not you care for her laws. You are obliged to accept her as she is and consequently all her end results. That is, a wall is a wall . . . etc, etc.' Good heavens! What do the laws of nature and arithmetic have to do with me if, for some reason, I don't happen to like those laws and that twice two is four? Naturally, I shan't break through that wall with my forehead, if in fact I don't have the strength, but I won't capitulate simply because I'm confronted with a stone wall and don't have the strength to break through.

As if a stone wall really did bring reassurance and really did have some message for the world, solely because it is twice two is four. Oh, absurdity of absurdities! How much better to understand everything, to be conscious of everything, of every impossibility, every stone wall; not to capitulate before a single one of those impossibilities or stone walls – if capitulating sickens you. To arrive by way of the most inexorable syllogisms at appalling conclusions on the eternal theme that somehow you are to blame even for that stone wall although once again it's abundantly clear that you're in no way to blame and consequently silently and impotently to grit your teeth and sink voluptuously into inertia, dreaming that there isn't even anyone for you to be angry with; that no object can be found and perhaps never will be; that it's all deception, juggling with facts, sharp practice, and that here there's nothing but a vile brew – we know neither what nor who – but despite all the uncertainties and juggling with facts you are still in pain and the less you know the more you ache!

IV

'Ha, ha, ha! Next you'll be finding pleasure even in a toothache!' you'll laugh out loud.

'What of it? There's pleasure even in toothache,' I'll reply. 'I once had toothache for a whole month; I know what it's like. People don't rage in silence, of course – they groan. But these aren't sincere groans – they are malicious groans and the whole point is in this malice. Through his groans the sufferer is expressing his pleasure. If he didn't find pleasure in them he wouldn't have started groaning. This is an excellent example, gentlemen, and I shall develop it. Firstly, in these groans the whole pointlessness of your pain – so humiliating for our consciousness – is expressed; the whole legitimacy of nature, for which you don't give a damn, of course, but from which you suffer all the same, while she doesn't. They express your awareness that even though your enemy is nowhere to be found you are in pain; your awareness that despite all the Wagenheims in the world[5] you are at the complete mercy of your teeth; that if someone should so wish, they could stop your teeth aching, but should they not so wish, they'll go on aching for another three months; and finally, that if you still disagree and carry on protesting, the only consolation that remains is to practise self-flagellation or hit the wall harder with your fists, but definitely no more than that. Well then, it's from these bloody insults, from these practical jokes carried out by persons unknown, that pleasure finally arrives, pleasure that sometimes reaches the peak of voluptuousness. I ask you, gentlemen, to listen sometimes to the groans of an educated man of the nineteenth century who is suffering from toothache, on the second or third day of his indisposition, when he's groaning quite differently from the way he did on the first day – that is, not simply because he has toothache; not like some coarse peasant, but rather like a man touched by enlightenment and European civilization groans, like a person "divorced from the soil and his native roots"[6] as they put it these days. His groans become something vile, viciously bad-tempered and continue all day and all night . . . And yet he himself knows perfectly well that his groans won't bring him any relief; better than anyone he knows that he is only irritating and overtaxing himself and everyone else for nothing. He knows that even the audience before whom he is performing with such fervour, and his whole family, are sick and tired of listening to him, that they don't believe him one bit and know in their heart of hearts that he could very well groan differently, in a more natural fashion, without the flourishes and affectation, and that he is merely indulging himself out of malice and bad humour. Well, the voluptuousness lies precisely in all this consciousness and disgrace. "I'm disturbing you," he says, "I'm lacerating your feelings, not letting anyone in the house sleep. Well, don't sleep, you ought to be experiencing every minute of my toothache. I'm no longer the hero I wanted to appear before, but merely a nasty fellow, a good-for-nothing. Very well, so be it! I'm delighted you've seen through me. Does it disgust you, listening to my ignoble groans? Well, let it disgust you; now I'm going to regale you with an even more disgusting roulade of groans . . ." Do you understand now, gentlemen? Well, one has to be highly developed and intensely aware to understand all the twists and turns of this voluptuous pleasure! Are you laughing? I'm absolutely delighted. Of course, my jokes, gentlemen, are in bad taste, uneven, muddled, lacking in confidence. But don't you see – that's because I have no self-respect. Can any thinking person have any kind of respect for himself?'

V

And can a man who has sought pleasure even in the actual consciousness of his degradation really have one atom of self-respect? I'm not speaking out of any feeling of unctuous remorse. And in general I never could bring myself to say: 'Forgive me, Papa, I won't do it again' – not because I was incapable of saying it – on the contrary. Perhaps it was precisely because I was all too capable of saying it – and do you know when? As if deliberately.

I used to get into awkward situations, just on those occasions when I wasn't to blame in any way. That was the most degrading part of it. On such occasions I would once again be deeply moved, I would repent, shed tears and of course I was fooling myself, although I was far from pretending. It was my heart that was somehow defiled . . . Here I couldn't even blame the laws of nature, although the laws of nature have constantly offended me all the same, more than anything else, my whole life.

I find it degrading to recall all this now and it was degrading at the time. You see, after a minute or so I would be bitterly reflecting that the whole thing was a lie, a lie, a loathsome, hypocritical lie, that is all these regrets, all this emotion, all these promises of regeneration. And if you ask why I tormented and mangled myself like that the answer is: because I was already terribly bored idly sitting around and so I indulged in all manner of capers. Really, that's how it was. If you observe yourselves a little more closely, gentlemen, you'll understand that it's so. I used to imagine adventures for myself, I invented a life, so that I could at least exist somehow. How many times, for example, have I taken offence, just like that, for no reason. And I myself knew very well that I had no reason to take offence and that I was putting it on, but I would work myself up to such a degree that in the end I really did feel offended. All my life I've been attracted to playing games like that, so that finally I lost all self-control. Once or even twice I wanted to force myself to fall in love. I really did suffer for it, gentlemen, I can assure you. Deep down within me I just cannot believe in my own suffering; there's a hint of self-mockery here, but I suffer all the same – and in an authentic, genuine fashion. I'm jealous, I lose all control over myself . . . And it all stems from boredom, gentlemen, from sheer boredom; I am crushed by inertia. After all, the immediate, legitimate, direct fruit of consciousness is inertia – that is, consciously sitting twiddling your thumbs. I've mentioned this before. I repeat, I repeat most emphatically: all spontaneous people and men of action are active because they are dull-witted and limited. What is the explanation for this? Well, it's like this: as a result of their limitations they take immediate and secondary causes for primary ones and are thus persuaded more quickly and easily than others that they have found an indisputable basis for whatever they do and so they are reassured. And that's the main thing. You see, in order to begin to act you must be completely sure in advance that there are no residual doubts whatsoever. But how can I, for example, reassure myself? Where are my primary causes on which I can take a stand, where are my foundations? Where shall I take them from? I practise thinking and consequently every primary cause immediately draws another in its wake, one that is even more primary, and so on *ad infinitum*. And that is precisely the essence of all thought processes or self-awareness. Again, this must therefore be the laws of nature. And what is the final result? Well, exactly the same. Remember that I was talking of revenge not so long ago. (You probably didn't get my meaning very well.) I said that a man avenges himself because he finds justice in it. That means he has found his primary cause, has found a basis for his actions, namely, justice. Therefore he is completely reassured on all counts and consequently takes his revenge calmly and successfully, convinced that what he is doing is just and honourable. But for the life of me I can see neither justice here nor virtue and consequently, if I start taking my revenge, it's really out of spite. Spite, of course, can overcome everything – all my doubts – and therefore it could quite successfully serve instead of a primary cause for the simple reason that it's not a cause. But what can I do if I don't even feel spite (after all, that's what I began with a short time ago)? Again, as a result of those damned laws of consciousness, my spite is subject to chemical decomposition. Just look – and the object vanishes into thin air, reasons evaporate, the culprit is nowhere to be found and the offence is no longer an offence but becomes destiny, something in the nature of a toothache for which no one is to blame and consequently there again remains the same way out – that is, banging your head against the wall so that it hurts even more. And so you give it up as a bad job because you've failed to find a primary cause. But just you try letting yourself be carried along blindly by your emotions, without reasoning, without primary cause, banishing your consciousness at least for the time being: hate or love – do anything but sit there not doing a stroke. The day after tomorrow, at the very latest, you will begin to despise yourself for having knowingly deceived yourself. The result is a soap bubble and inertia. You see, gentlemen, perhaps I only consider myself an intelligent person because all my life I've never been capable of starting or finishing anything. All right, so I'm a windbag, a harmless, tiresome windbag, as all of us are. But what can one do about it if the direct and sole purpose of any intelligent man is idle chatter, that is, deliberately milling the wind?

VI

Oh, if only it were simply out of laziness that I did nothing! Heavens, how I should have respected myself then! I should have respected myself precisely because I was at least capable of being lazy. At least I should have possessed one positive quality of which I myself could have been certain. Question: what is he? Answer: a lazy devil. Of course, it would be really most pleasant to have heard that said of oneself.

It implies something positively defined, that there's something to be said about me. 'Lazy devil!' Why, that's a rank and a calling, that's a career. Don't joke about it – it's true. Then I should by rights be a member of the most exclusive club and my sole occupation would be nursing my self-esteem. I once knew a gentleman who all his life prided himself on being a great connoisseur of Château Lafite. He considered this his own positive merit and never doubted himself. He died, not so much with an easy conscience but with a triumphant one and he was absolutely right. And I should have chosen a career for myself at the time: I would have been a loafer and a glutton – but not a simple one, rather one who for example empathizes with all that is sublime and beautiful. How do you like that? I was haunted by visions of it long ago. This 'sublime and beautiful' is a real pain in the neck now that I'm forty. But that's because I'm forty – but then, oh then it would have been different! I should at once have sought out a suitable sphere of activity for myself, namely, toasting the health of all that is sublime and beautiful. I would have seized every opportunity of first shedding a tear into my glass and then draining it in honour of the sublime and beautiful. Then I would have transformed everything in the world into the sublime and beautiful; I should have sought out the sublime and beautiful in the most revolting, indisputable filth. I should have become as lachrymose as a wet sponge. For example, the artist Ge[7] has painted a picture and I immediately drink the health of that artist Ge, the painter of that picture, because I am a lover of all that is sublime and beautiful. An author has written 'For your satisfaction'; immediately I toast the health of 'your satisfaction' since I love all that is sublime and beautiful. I insist on being respected for that and I shall hunt down anyone who fails to show me respect. Thus I live peacefully and die in triumph. Why, that's delightful, simply delightful! And then I should have developed such a paunch, cultivated such a triple chin, produced such a purple nose for myself that any passer-by would exclaim on looking at me: 'Well, there's a fine fellow! He's really got something about him!' Say what you like, gentlemen, it's extremely pleasant to hear such tributes in this negative age of ours.

VII

But all these are golden dreams. Oh, do tell me who first announced, who first proclaimed, that man only does vile things because he doesn't know his own true interests; that if he were enlightened, if his eyes were to be opened to his real, normal interests he would immediately cease doing vile things and at once become virtuous and honourable; since, once he is enlightened and understands what will truly benefit him, he will see that his own best interests lie in doing good; that since it's common knowledge that no man can act knowingly against his own best interests he would necessarily do good. Oh, the child! Oh, the pure, innocent babe! In the first place when did man, in all these thousands of years, ever act solely in his own best interests? What about the millions of cases that bear witness to the fact that people *knowingly*, that is, while fully comprehending their own best interests, relegating them to the background and following a different, uncertain and risky path, not because they are being forced to do that by anyone or anything, but simply as if reluctant to follow the appointed path, stubbornly and wilfully choose to forge ahead along another difficult and absurd path, seeking it in almost total darkness? This can only mean that for men this obstinacy and wilfulness was in actual fact more agreeable to them than any kind of personal advantage . . . Advantage! What is advantage? Would you care to volunteer an absolutely exact definition of what human advantage consists of? And what if it should *sometimes* happen that human advantage not only might, but even must lie precisely in man desiring, in different cases, what is bad for himself and not to his advantage? And if this is so, if such things are at all possible, then the whole rule goes to blazes. What do you think – can such cases occur? You laugh? Well, laugh, gentlemen, but just answer me this: are human advantages calculated with perfect accuracy? Are there not some that not only have not been classified but cannot even be classified at all? After all, gentlemen, as far as I know, you have deduced your whole register of human advantages by taking averages from statistics and scientifico-economic formulae. And since your advantages are prosperity, wealth, freedom, peace and so on, and so on, so that anyone who, for example, were to act openly and knowingly against the whole register would, in your opinion and in mine too of course, be an obscurantist or a complete madman – isn't that so? But the really amazing thing is surely this: how does it always happen that all these statisticians, sages and lovers of the human race, when enumerating human advantages, invariably omit a particular one? They don't even take it into account as it should be taken and on this the entire calculation depends. In effect, there would be no great harm in taking this advantage and adding it to their list. But the snag is that this abstruse advantage doesn't fit into any classification, or cannot be accommodated in any list. For instance, I have a friend . . . Oh, gentlemen! He's a friend of yours too and in fact to whom is he not a friend? When he undertakes to do something this gentleman will immediately expound to you, lucidly and grandiloquently, exactly how he should proceed, according to the laws of truth and logic. And that's not all: he'll talk to you with enthusiasm and passion about true, normal human interests; he'll scornfully sneer at those short-sighted fools who understand neither their own interests nor the true meaning of virtue; and then, exactly a quarter of an hour later, without any sudden, outside mediation, but rather prompted by some inner impulse which is stronger that all his interests, he'll take a completely different tack, that is to say, he'll blatantly go against what he was just saying: against the laws of reason and against his own best interests – in short, against everything . . . I'm warning you that my friend is a collective person, so it's rather difficult to pin the blame on him individually. Now that's just the point, gentlemen: doesn't there exist, in fact, something that is dearer to almost everyone than his own very best interests or (not to violate logic) there exists one most advantageous advantage (to be precise, the omitted one of which we were talking just now) which is more important and advantageous than any other advantage and for the sake of which man, should the need arise, is ready to oppose all the laws, that is, reason, honour, peace, prosperity – in short, all these fine and useful things, provided he attains this primary, most advantageous advantage which is dearest of all to him?

'Well,' you'll interrupt, 'they're advantages all the same.' If you don't mind, we'll clarify matters – yes, we're not talking about plays upon words, but the fact that this advantage is remarkable precisely because it destroys all our classifications and is constantly demolishing all systems devised by lovers of humanity for the happiness of the human race. In short, it interferes with everything. But before I give a name to this advantage I want to compromise myself personally and therefore I boldly declare that all these fine systems, all these theories that explain to humanity its best, normal interests, and assert that by striving out of necessity to attain them, it will immediately become virtuous and noble, are in my opinion pure sophistry! Oh yes, sophistry! You see, even to affirm this theory of the regeneration of the entire human race by means of this systematic classification of its own personal advantages is, in my opinion, almost the same as affirming with Buckle,[8] for example, that civilization softens man and therefore he becomes less bloodthirsty and less inclined to wage war. He appears to argue it very logically. But man is so partial to systems and abstract conclusions that he is ready deliberately to distort the truth, ready neither to hear nor see anything, only as long as he can justify his logic. That's why I take this as an example, because it is an all too striking one. Just take a look around you: blood is flowing in rivers and in such a jolly way you'd think it was champagne. There's your entire nineteenth century, in which Buckle lived too. There's your Napoleon – both the great Napoleon and the present-day one.[9] There's your North America[10] the everlasting Union. Finally, there's your grotesque Schleswig-Holstein . . .[11] And what does civilization soften in us? Civilization develops in man only the many-sidedness of his sensations and decidedly nothing more. And through the development of this many-sidedness man may advance still further to the stage where he will find pleasure in bloodshed. Well, that's already happened to him. Have you noticed that the most refined bloodshedders have almost invariably been highly civilized gentlemen, to whom all those different Attilas and Stenka Razins could not have held a candle. And if they don't arrest your attention as powerfully as Attila[12] and Stenka Razin,[13] that's precisely because you meet with them so often, they are too commonplace and too familiar. At all events, if as a result of civilization man hasn't grown more bloodthirsty, he has certainly become viler in his quest for blood than before. Formerly he saw justice in bloodshed and exterminated those he needed to with an easy conscience. But nowadays, although we consider bloodshed something abhorrent, we still participate in it – and more than ever. Which is worse? – that you must decide for yourselves. They say that Cleopatra[14] (apologies for taking an example from Roman history) was fond of sticking gold pins into the bosoms of her slave girls, taking keen delight in their screams and contortions. You will say that this happened in relatively barbarous times; that today too times are still barbarous because (also relatively speaking) we still stick pins into people; and that even now, although man has learned to see more clearly than in barbarous times, he's a long way from *accustoming* himself to act as science and reason dictate. For all that you are absolutely convinced that man is bound to grow accustomed once certain bad old habits have been discarded and when science and common sense have fully re-educated and directed human nature along normal lines. You are convinced that man will then, *of his own accord*, cease making mistakes and – so to speak – willy-nilly refuse to divorce his volition from his normal interests. And that's not all: you say that then science itself will teach man (although in my opinion this is already a luxury) that in actual fact he possesses neither will nor whims and never did have them and that he is nothing more than a sort of piano key or organ stop; and, what is more, that there do exist in this world the laws of nature, so that whatever he does is not of his own volition at all, but exists according to the laws of nature. Consequently these laws of nature need only to be revealed and man will no longer be responsible for his actions and life will be extremely easy for him. All human actions, it goes without saying, will then be calculated according to these laws, mathematically, like a logarithm table, reaching 108,000 and entered in a directory. Better still, certain orthodox publications will appear, rather like our modern encyclopaedic dictionaries, in which everything will be so accurately calculated and specified that there will no longer be either independent actions or adventures in this world.

And then – it's still you who maintain this – a new political economy will appear on the scene, ready-made and also calculated with mathematical precision, so that in a flash all conceivable questions will vanish, simply because all conceivable replies to them will have been provided. Then the Crystal Palace[15] will be erected. Then . . . well, the Golden Age will dawn. Of course, it's quite impossible to guarantee (it's me speaking now) that things won't be incredibly boring, for example (because what will there be left to do once everything is calculated according to tables?); but, on the other hand, everything will be extraordinarily rational. Of course, when you're bored you can think up all sorts of things! After all, it's from boredom that gold pins are stuck into people, but none of that would matter. The bad thing is (and again it's me speaking) that then – who knows? – people might be glad even of gold pins. Man is so stupid, phenomenally stupid. I mean to say, he may not be so completely stupid, but then he's so ungrateful that you couldn't find another like him, even if you were to look hard. For example, I wouldn't be in the least surprised if some gentleman of dishonourable – better, of reactionary and mocking – appearance were suddenly to spring up from nowhere amidst this universal good sense, stand hands on hips and tell every one of us: well, gentlemen, why don't we get rid of this good sense once and for all by giving it a good kick, just so that we can send all these logarithms to hell and once again be able to live according to our own foolish will? That wouldn't be so bad, but the really galling thing is that he would undoubtedly find followers: that's the way men are fashioned. And all this for the most trivial reason which, one would think, is hardly worth mentioning: to be precise, because man, whoever he may be, has always and everywhere preferred to act as he chooses and not at all as his reason or personal advantage dictate; indeed, one can act contrary to one's own best interests and sometimes it's *absolutely imperative* to do so (that's my idea). One's own free, independent desire, one's own whims, however unbridled, one's fantasy, sometimes inflamed to the point of madness – all this is precisely that same, invariably omitted, most advantageous of advantages which cannot be accommodated within any classification and because of which all systems and theories are constantly consigned to the devil. And where on earth did all those sages get the idea that man needs some kind of virtuous, some kind of normal desire? How did they come to imagine that man categorically needs rational, advantageous desire? All man needs is *independent* volition, whatever that independence might cost and wherever it might lead. Anyway, the devil only knows what volition is.

VIII

'Ha, ha, ha! Well, if you like, essentially there's no such thing as volition!' you interrupt with your guffaws. 'By now science has made such advances in anatomizing man that we know that volition and so-called free will are nothing other than . . .'

'Hold on, gentlemen, that's how I myself wanted to begin. I do confess that I even took fright. I was just about to shout out loud that the devil knows what volition depends on – and we may perhaps thank God for that – and then I remembered about science and I . . . quietened down. At that point you joined in. As it happens, if they do in fact discover one day a formula for all our desires and caprices – that is, what they depend on, exactly from what laws they originate, exactly how they are disseminated, to what they are aspiring in one case or the other, and so on and so on, that's to say a real mathematical formula, then man will very likely at once stop desiring anything and most probably cease to exist altogether. What is the point of desiring by numbers? What's more, he would immediately change from a man into an organ stop or something like that. Because what is man without his volition but a stop on a barrel-organ cylinder? What do you think? Consider the probabilities – could it happen or couldn't it?'

'Hm,' you opine, 'for the main part our desires are erroneous because of an erroneous view of what is in our own best interest. The reason why we sometimes desire pure nonsense is that in our stupidity we see in that nonsense the easiest route to achieving some kind of previously assumed advantage . . . Well, when all this is explained and calculated on paper (which is highly possible since it is base and senseless to believe in advance that there are certain laws of nature that man will never discover) then of course there will no longer be any of these so-called desires. You see, if volition should ever come to be completely identified with reason, then we shall of course reason and not desire, precisely because it's obviously impossible to *desire* nonsense while preserving our reason and thus knowingly go against reason and desire what is harmful . . . And since all volition, all reasoning, can actually be tabulated, because one fine day they will discover the laws of our so-called free will, then, in all seriousness, they will be able to draw up some kind of table, ensuring that we really shall desire in accordance with that table. You see, if at some time it could be calculated and proven to me, for example, that if I cocked a snook at someone, it was because I could not help it and that I was bound to stick my finger up that way, then how could there be anything left in me that could be called *free*, especially if I'm a scholar and have attended a science course somewhere? In that case I'd be able to calculate the next thirty years of my life in advance; in brief, if that's how things were to be arranged, there would of course be nothing left for us to do. We'd have to accept it all the same. And in general we should have to keep repeating to ourselves, without flagging for one moment, that without fail, at certain moments and in certain circumstances, nature does not stop to ask our permission; that we must accept her as she is and not as we imagine her to be; and that if we really are speeding towards tables and directories and . . . well, even towards test tubes, then what can we do but accept the test tube too! Otherwise the test tube will be accepted without us . . .

'Oh yes, sir – that's just where the snag is as far as I'm

concerned! Forgive me, gentlemen, for philosophizing away like this – that comes from forty years underground! Allow me to indulge in a little fantasizing. You see, gentlemen: reason is a good thing, there's no denying it, but reason is only reason and satisfies only man's rational faculty, whereas volition is a manifestation of the whole of life – and by that I mean the whole of life, together with reason and all the headscratching that goes with it. And even if, in this manifestation, our life frequently turns out to be rubbish, it is still life and not simply the extraction of a square root. As for me, I quite naturally want to live in order to satisfy my whole capacity for living and not solely to satisfy my capacity for reasoning, which is only one-twentieth of my entire capacity for living. What does reason know? Reason only knows what it has managed to discover (the rest, perhaps, it will never discover; that's little comfort, but why not say it outright?), whereas human nature acts as a whole, with everything it comprises, conscious or unconscious; it may talk nonsense, yet it lives. I suspect, gentlemen, that you're looking at me with pity; you keep repeating that an enlightened and intellectually mature person – in short, man as he will be in the future – cannot knowingly desire something that is not to his advantage and that this is mathematics. I entirely agree, it really is mathematics. But I repeat to you for the hundredth time that there is one case and only one, when man may deliberately and consciously desire something that is downright harmful even stupid, even extremely stupid, and that is: to *have the right* to desire what is even extremely stupid and not to be duty bound to desire only what is intelligent. You see, this height of stupidity is your caprice, gentlemen, and in fact might be more advantageous to us than anything else on earth, especially in certain circumstances. But in particular it can be more advantageous than any other advantage even when it obviously does us harm and contradicts the soundest conclusions of our reasoning about advantage, because at any rate it preserves what is most precious and most important to us, and that is our personality and our individuality. In fact some would claim that this is in fact more precious than anything else to man. Of course, volition may coincide with reason if it so wishes, especially if it is not abused but used in moderation; this is useful and occasionally even laudable. But very often and for the main part volition is directly and obstinately at loggerheads with reason and . . . and . . . do you know that this too is useful and sometimes even highly laudable? Let's suppose, gentlemen, that man is not stupid. (Actually, it's absolutely impossible to say this about him, for the sole reason that if he's stupid then who is clever?) But if he's not stupid, he's monstrously ungrateful all the same. Phenomenally ungrateful. I even think that the best definition of man is this: he's a two-legged creature and an ingrate. But that's not all – that isn't even his principal shortcoming; his principal shortcoming is his constant improper behaviour, constant from the time of the Flood to the Schleswig-Holstein period of human history. Improper behaviour and therefore lack of reason, since it has long been known that irrationality originates from nothing else than improper behaviour. Just cast your eye over the history of mankind – and what do you see? Is it grand? All right, then let's say it's grand. Just think how much the Colossus of Rhodes[16] alone is worth! It's not for nothing that Mr Anayevsky[17] testifies that whereas some people claim it is the work of human hands, others maintain that it was created by nature herself. Variety? Well, perhaps even variety. Consider only the ceremonial uniforms, military and civilian of all nations, at all times and think what they must be worth! And if you include civil service uniforms – well, the mind boggles! Not a single historian would cope with them. Monotony? Well, I suppose monotony too. Fighting and fighting – they're fighting now, they fought before and will fight again.

'You must agree it's already excessively monotonous. In brief, you can say anything you like about world history, anything that could be conceived only by the most disordered imagination. Only one thing cannot be said, however – that it's in any way rational. You'd choke on the first word. And there's another thing that keeps cropping up: such moral and sensible people are always appearing in life, such sages and lovers of mankind who have made it their lifetime's ambition to conduct themselves as decently and sensibly as possible, to enlighten their neighbours, strictly speaking, to prove to them in effect that it really is possible to live both morally and rationally in this world. What then? We know very well that sooner or later many of these philanthropists have, in their twilight years, betrayed themselves by committing some foolish act, sometimes of the most scandalous variety. Now I ask you: what can one expect of man, as a creature endowed with such strange qualities? Yes, shower him with all earthly blessings, immerse him so completely in happiness that the bubbles dance on the surface of his happiness, as though on water; grant him such economic prosperity that he will have absolutely nothing else to do but sleep, eat gingerbread and concern himself with the continuance of world history – and that man, out of sheer ingratitude, out of sheer devilment, will even then do the dirty on you. He will even put his gingerbread at risk and deliberately set his heart on the most pernicious trash, the most uneconomical nonsense solely in order to alloy all this positive good sense with his pernicious, fantastic element. It's precisely his fantastic dreams, his gross stupidity, that he wants to cling to, solely to convince himself (as if this were absolutely essential) that people are still people and not piano keys upon which the laws of nature themselves are not only playing with their own hands, but threatening to persist in playing until nothing can be desired that is not tabulated in the directory. And that's not all: even if it were really the case that man turned out to be a piano key and if this were to be proven to him even by the natural sciences and mathematics – even then he wouldn't see reason but would deliberately do something to contradict this, out of sheer ingratitude, just to have things his own way. And in any situation where he didn't have the means to carry this out he would create chaos and destruction and devise various modes of suffering and still insist on having things his own way! He'll unleash his curse on the world and since only man is able to curse (that's his privilege, which principally distinguishes him from the other animals) then, through cursing alone he might achieve his object and convince himself that he's a man and not a piano key! If you say that even all this – the chaos, gloom and imprecations – can be calculated according to tables, so that the mere possibility of advance calculations will put a stop to everything and reason would prevail – in that case man would deliberately go insane in order to be rid of reason and still have things his own way. I believe in this, I'm prepared to vouch for it, because this whole human business would seem in fact to consist only in this, that man should always be proving to himself that he's a man and not an organ stop! He's always proved it, however much it takes – he's proved it even by becoming a troglodyte. And after that how can one fail to transgress, to applaud that this has not yet come about and that meanwhile volition depends on the devil knows what . . .

You will shout out to me (if you still deign to favour me with your shouts) that here in fact no one is trying to deprive me of my free will; that all they're doing is fuss: about how to arrange things so that my will should of its own accord coincide with my normal interests, with the laws of nature and with arithmetic.

'Ah, gentlemen! What will become of your will once the whole business ends up with tables and arithmetic, when only twice two is four is in demand? Twice two will make four without my willing it. So much for your will!'

IX

Of course I'm joking, gentlemen, and I myself know that I'm not joking very successfully, but really, you mustn't take everything as a joke. Perhaps I'm joking with clenched teeth. Gentlemen, I'm tormented by various questions; answer them for me. For example, here you are, wanting to wean man from his old habits and correct his will in conformity with the demands of science and common sense. But how do you know that man not only can, but *must* be modified this way? On what grounds do you conclude that man's volition *must*, of necessity, be corrected that way? In short, how do you know that such a correction will really benefit man? All said and done, why are you so *utterly* convinced that not opposing man's real, normal advantages, which are guaranteed by the deductions of reason and arithmetic, is really always to his advantage and is a law for all mankind? Surely this is as yet only your supposition. Let's assume it's a law of logic, but perhaps not a law at all for mankind. You might be thinking I'm insane, gentlemen. Allow me to make one proviso. I agree that man is, above all, a predominantly creative animal, condemned consciously to strive towards a goal and to engage in the art of engineering, that is, eternally, unceasingly constructing a road for himself *wherever it may lead*. And the reason why he perhaps sometimes wants to swerve to the side is precisely that he is *condemned* to follow that path and also, perhaps, because however stupid your plain man of action may be in general, he will sometimes get the idea into his head that this path, as it turns out, almost always leads *wherever it's going to lead*, and that the important thing is not where it's leading, but that it should lead somewhere and that our well-behaved child, scorning the art of engineering, should not surrender to that ruinous idleness which, as we all know, is the mother of all vices. Man loves to construct and lay down roads, no question about it. But why is he so passionately fond of destruction and chaos? Tell me that!

But here I myself would like to say a few words about that in particular. Isn't man perhaps so passionately fond of destruction and chaos (and there's no disputing that he's sometimes very fond of them, that really is the case) that he himself instinctively fears achieving his goal and completing the building in course of erection? How do you know – perhaps he only likes the building from a distance and not at all at close quarters; perhaps he only likes building it and not living in it, leaving it afterwards *aux animaux domestiques*,[18] such as ants, sheep, etc. Now these ants' tastes are completely different. They have one amazing building of this type, which is eternally indestructible – the anthill.

The worthy ants began with an anthill and they'll most probably finish with an anthill, which does much credit to their persistence and positive outlook. But man is a superficial and unseemly creature and perhaps, like a chess player, is fond only of the actual process of achieving his goal rather than the goal itself. And who knows (no one can say for sure), perhaps the whole goal towards which mankind is striving in this world consists solely in the uninterrupted process of achievement – in other words, in life itself and specifically in the goal which, needless to say, can be nothing other than twice two is four – in other words, a formula; but twice two is four is no longer life, gentlemen, but the beginning of death . . . At least, man has always somehow been afraid of this twice two is four and I'm still afraid of it. Let's suppose that man does nothing but seek out this twice two is four formula, sails across oceans, devoting his life to the quest but never really finding it – God, he's afraid of it somehow! You see, he feels that once he's found it there'll be nothing left to look for. When they finish work, labourers at least take their money and off they go to the pub and end up at the police station. Well, that's a good week's work. But where can man go? At all events one can observe something uncomfortable about him every time he achieves his goal. He loves progressing towards his goal but not quite reaching it, and this of course is terribly funny. In short, man is a comically fashioned creature and evidently there's a joke behind all this. Twice two is four is nevertheless an intolerable thing. Twice two is four is, in my opinion, nothing more than a damned cheek. Twice two is four looks on smugly, hands on hips, stands in your path and defies you. I agree that twice two is four is an excellent thing, but if we're going to praise everything then twice two is five can sometimes be a most charming little thing as well!

And why are you so soundly, so solemnly convinced that only the normal and the positive – in brief, convinced that prosperity alone is advantageous to man? Can't reason make mistakes about advantages? Perhaps prosperity isn't the only thing that man loves? Perhaps he likes suffering just as much? Perhaps suffering is just as advantageous to him as prosperity? Sometimes man loves suffering intensely, passionately – and that's a fact. In this instance it's no good consulting world history. Just ask yourself, if you're a man with any experience of life. As for my personal opinion, to love only prosperity is even somehow unseemly. Whether it's a good thing or a bad thing, smashing something is occasionally very pleasant too.

I'm not campaigning for suffering, or for prosperity. I'm advocating . . . my own caprice and that it should be guaranteed me when the need arises. In vaudevilles, for example, suffering is taboo, I know that. In the Crystal Palace it's unthinkable: suffering is doubt, negation, and what kind of Crystal Palace could it be where there's room for doubt? And yet I'm convinced that man will never renounce true suffering, that is, destruction and chaos. Suffering – yes, that's surely the sole cause of consciousness. Although I did maintain at the beginning that, in my opinion, suffering is man's greatest misfortune, I know that man loves it and would not exchange it for any gratification whatsoever. Consciousness, for example, is infinitely superior to twice two is four. After twice two is four, of course there'll be nothing left, not only to do but even to discover. All that would then be possible would be to shut off your five senses and bury yourself in meditation. Well, even if you arrive at the same result with consciousness, that is, there won't be anything for you to do either, but at least you could sometimes give yourself a good flogging, which is stimulating all the same. This may be retrograde, but it's still better than nothing.

X

You believe in the Crystal Palace, eternally indestructible – that is, in something at which you can neither stick out your tongue nor cock a snook on the sly. Well, perhaps the reason I fear this edifice is that it is made of crystal and eternally indestructible and because you cannot even furtively stick your tongue out at it.

So, you see: if instead of a palace there were a hen house and if it started raining I might perhaps creep into the hen house to avoid getting soaked, but I would never take the hen house for a palace, out of gratitude for protecting me from the rain. You're laughing, you're even telling me that in this case it doesn't matter whether it's a hen house or a mansion. Yes, I reply, if one's only aim in life is not getting wet.

But what can I do if I've taken it into my head that this is not the sole purpose of living and that if one has to live it might as well be in a mansion. That is my volition, that is my desire. You'll only rid me of it by changing my desire. Well, change it, tempt me with something else, give me another ideal. But in the meantime I shan't take a hen house for a palace. It might even be that the Crystal Palace is a sham, that it's not provided for by the laws of nature and that I only invented it as a result of my stupidity and certain outmoded, irrational habits of our generation. But what's it to do with me if it's not provided for? Isn't it all the same, so long as it exists in my desires – better, if it exists as long as my desires exist? Perhaps you're laughing again? Well, by all means laugh. I'll put up with your derision but I still won't say I'm full when I'm hungry. For all that, I know that I'll never settle for compromise, for a constantly recurring zero simply because it exists according to the laws of nature and *in actual fact* exists. I shall not accept as the crown of my desires a big tenement block with flats for impoverished tenants on thousand-year leases, with the dentist Wagenheim's name on the sign board for emergencies. Do away with my desires, eradicate my ideals, show me something better and I will follow you. You'll probably say that it's not worth getting involved; but in that case I could give you the same reply. This is a serious discussion; if you don't want to honour me with your attention I shan't come begging for it. I have my underground.

Meanwhile I carry on living and desiring – may my hand fall off if I carry one brick to that tenement block! Ignore the fact that just now I rejected the Crystal Palace for the sole reason that it would be impossible to stick one's tongue out at it. By no means was I saying this because I'm so fond of sticking out my tongue. Perhaps I was only angry because, out of all your buildings, not one edifice at which you couldn't stick out your tongue has been found up to now. On the contrary, I would let my tongue be cut off, from sheer gratitude, if only that building could be so constructed that I would never again have the urge to stick it out again. What does it concern me if it were impossible to construct and that we had to content ourselves with tenement blocks? So why was I created with such desires? Could I possibly have been created solely and simply to reach the conclusion that my whole make-up is nothing but a swindle? Can that be the whole purpose? I don't believe it.

However, do you know what? I'm convinced that underground people like me must be kept under strict control. They might well be capable of sitting in their underground for forty years without uttering one word, but the moment they emerge into the light of day and break their silence they just talk and talk and talk . . .

XI

To sum up, gentlemen: the best thing is to do nothing! Better conscious inertia! So, long live the underground! Although I may have said that I envy the normal man with all the rancour of which I'm capable, I wouldn't care to be him, in the situation in which I see him (although I shan't stop envying him all the same. No, no, in any event the underground is more advantageous!). There one can at least . . . Ah! You see, here again I'm lying! I'm lying because I myself know, as sure as twice two is four, that it's not the underground that's better in any way, but something else, something completely different, which I long for but which I just cannot find! To hell with the underground! Even this would be better: if I myself could believe just a little of all that I've written now! I solemnly assure you, gentlemen, that I don't believe one word, not a single word of what I've just scribbled here. I mean to say, perhaps I really do believe it but at the same time, I don't know why, I feel and suspect I'm lying like a bootmaker.

'So why have you written all this?' you ask me.

'Well, I'd like to shut you away for forty years with nothing at all to do and then come and visit you after forty years to see what had become of you. Surely a man can't be left alone for forty years with nothing to do?'

'But isn't that disgraceful, isn't that humiliating!' you may possibly ask me, scornfully wagging your heads. 'You thirst for life and yet you try to solve life's problems with muddled logic. And how tiresome, how impudent your outbursts are – and at the same time how frightened you are! You talk nonsense and are happy with it. You come out with insolent remarks, yet you constantly fear for the consequences and apologize. You assure us that you are afraid of nothing yet you come crawling for our approval. You assure us that your teeth are clenched and at the same time you crack jokes in order to amuse us. You know that your jokes are not very witty, but you're evidently satisfied with their literary merit. Perhaps you really have had to suffer at times, but you have no respect whatsoever for your suffering. There is even truth in you, but no integrity; out of the pettiest vanity you carry your truth to the marketplace to be paraded in public and put to shame . . . You really do want to say something, but from fear you conceal your last word, since you haven't the resolve to say it, only craven impudence. You boast of your consciousness, but all you do is vacillate, since although your brain is functioning your heart is darkened by depravity and without a pure heart there can never be full, authentic consciousness. And how importunate you are, how pushy, how pretentious! Lies, lies and more lies!'

Of course, I've just now invented all these words of yours myself. This too comes from the underground. I've been listening to these words of yours through a chink for forty years on end. I thought them up myself – you see, there was nothing else for me to think up. So it's not surprising they were learnt by heart and acquired literary form . . .

But surely, surely you're not so gullible as to imagine that I'm going to publish all this and, what's more, give it to you to read? And I have another problem on my hands: why do I in fact address you as 'gentlemen', why do I treat you as if you really were my readers? Such confessions as I intend committing to paper don't get printed or given to others to read. At least, I don't have sufficient firmness of purpose for that, nor do I consider it necessary. Don't you see? A certain fantasy has entered my head and at all events I wish to realize it. Now this is what it's all about.

In every man's memories there are certain things that he will not reveal to everyone but only to his friends. And there are things that he will not even disclose to his friends, only to himself and even then under a veil of secrecy. But, finally, there are things that he's afraid of divulging even to himself and every decent man has quite an accumulation of these. It might even be the case that the more respectable a person is the more he will have of them. At least, only recently I decided to recall some of my earlier adventures which up to now I had always passed over with a certain degree of uneasiness. But now, when not only am I recalling them but have even decided to write them down, what I really wish to put to the test is: can one be perfectly honest with oneself and not be afraid of the whole truth? Apropos of this I would point out that Heine claims that true autobiographies are almost impossible and that a man will most certainly lie about himself.[19] In his opinion, Rousseau, for example, undoubtedly lied about himself in his *Confessions* – even lied deliberately, out of vanity. I'm convinced that Heine is right; I can understand perfectly well how one can sometimes accuse onself of all sorts of crimes solely out of vanity and I even understand very well the nature of that vanity. But Heine was passing judgement on a man who was making a *public* confession. But I'm writing for myself alone and declare once and for all that if I'm writing as if I'm addressing readers, then it's purely for show, since it's easier writing like that. It's only a form, an empty form. I shall never have any readers. I've already said as much . . .

I don't want to be restricted in any way in editing my notes. I shan't introduce any order or system. Whatever I happen to remember I shall write down.

But here you might start quibbling and ask: if you're not counting on having any readers then why do you make such compacts with yourself – on paper, what's more; that is to say, that you won't be introducing any order or system, that you'll just write down what you happen to remember, and so on and so on? Why are you explaining all this, why all these excuses?

'Well, you just think,' I reply.

There's a whole psychology here, however. Perhaps it's that

I'm simply a coward. But perhaps it's because I'm deliberately imagining I have an audience before me so that I conduct myself more fittingly when I come to write things down. There could be a thousand reasons.

But there's something else: why, why exactly do I want to write? If it's not for the public then couldn't I very well commit everything to memory without putting pen to paper?

Quite so; but it will turn out somehow grander on paper. There's something inspirational about it, one can be more self-critical, and it makes for better style. Besides, perhaps by writing things down I really shall find relief. Only today, for example, I'm particularly oppressed by some very ancient memory. It came vividly to mind only recently and since then has plagued me like some tiresome musical motif that one can't get rid of. But meanwhile I must get rid of it. I have hundreds of similar memories, but at times one of them stands out from the hundreds and weighs heavily on me. For some reason I believe that by writing it down I shall rid myself of it. So why not try?

Lastly, I'm bored, I do nothing the whole time. Writing things down is really work of a kind. They say that work makes a man good and honest. Well, at least there's a chance.

Just now it's snowing – almost wet, yellowish, dirty snow. Yesterday it snowed too and the day before that. I think that the wet snow reminded me of that incident which refuses to stop pestering me. So, let this be a tale apropos of the wet snow.[20]

II

Apropos of the Wet Snow

When from error's murky ways,
I freed your fallen soul,
With burning words of exhortation.
When, filled with profound torment
You wrung your hands and cursed
All-ensnaring vice.
When with memory punishing
Your conscience so unmindful,
You told me the tale
Of all that was before me.
Then suddenly, hiding your face,
Overcome with shame and horror,
Indignant and shaken,
You tearfully resolved . . .
Etc, etc, etc . . .[21]
From the poetry of N. A. Nekrasov

At that time I was no more than twenty-four years old. Even then my life was gloomy, chaotic and wildly lonely. I didn't socialize with anyone, I even avoided conversations and withdrew further and further into my corner. At work, in the office, I even tried not to look at anyone and I realized perfectly well that my colleagues not only regarded me as a crank – and this is how it always struck me – but seemed to look on me with a kind of loathing. I used to wonder: why does no one else but me get the impression he's looked upon with loathing? One of our office clerks had a repulsive, extremely pock-marked face, rather like a criminal's, even. With such a repulsive face like that, I thought, I would never have dared look at anyone. Another clerk had a uniform that was so tatty there was a nasty smell if you went near him. And yet neither of these two gentlemen was embarrassed, neither on account of his clothes nor his face, nor on moral grounds, so to speak. Neither one of them imagined for one moment that he was being looked upon with loathing; and if they did imagine that, they didn't care one rap, as long as their superiors didn't deign to look at them. Now it's abundantly clear to me that because of my unbounded vanity, and the demands I made upon myself, I very often looked upon myself with furious dissatisfaction that amounted to disgust and consequently I mentally attributed my own attitude to everyone else. For example, I hated my face, I found it vile, I even suspected that it had a kind of base expression and so whenever I appeared at the office I suffered agonies in attempting to behave as independently as possible, to ensure that they didn't suspect me of baseness and to give my face the most dignified expression possible. 'Well, what if my face *is* unsightly,' I thought, 'it doesn't matter as long as it has a noble, expressive and above all *extremely* intelligent look.' But I knew without any doubt, I was painfully aware, that my face could never express all these perfections. But what was worse than anything, I found it positively stupid. I would have been quite happy to settle for intelligence. I would even have been content with a base expression, as long as my face struck people as awfully intelligent at the same time.

Needless to say, I hated all the office clerks from first to last and despised them all, yet at the same time I was also somehow afraid of them. Sometimes, it happened that I would even rate them as superior to myself. It was all very sudden: one moment I would despise them and the next I'd rate them superior to myself. A cultured, self-respecting person cannot be vain without making unlimited demands on himself and without at other times despising himself to the point of hatred. But whether I despised them, or classed them as my superiors, practically at every encounter I would lower my eyes. I even used to make experiments to discover whether I could bear someone – whoever it might be – staring at me, and I was invariably the first to look down. This tormented me to distraction. Also, the fear of appearing ridiculous made me ill and so I slavishly followed routine in everything that had to do with outward appearances.

Enthusiastically, I fell into the common rut and with my heart and soul feared the least sign of eccentricity in myself. But how was I to keep it up? I was painfully cultivated, as any cultivated man of our times should be. But they were a dim-witted lot, each like the other as a flock of sheep. Perhaps I was the only clerk in the whole office who always looked upon himself as a coward and slave and that's precisely why I felt I was cultivated. But not only did I appear to be, in actual fact I *was* a coward and a slave. I say that without the least embarrassment. Every self-respecting man of our time is, and is bound to be, a coward and a slave. That's his normal condition. Of that I'm deeply convinced. That's how he's fashioned, that's what he's created for. And it is not simply in our time, as a consequence of certain random events, but it's generally true at all times that any self-respecting man is bound to be a coward and a slave. This is a law of nature that applies to every decent person in this world. Even if one of them happens to put on a show of bravery over something, he shouldn't take any comfort from it or get carried away, he'll still make a fool of himself in front of others. This is the only and eternal outcome. Only asses and cross-breeds try to appear brave and even then to a certain extent. But it's not worth paying attention to them, since they don't matter one little bit.

At that time one other thing tormented me – to be precise, no one was like me, nor was I like anyone else. 'I am one person and they are *everybody*,' I thought, becoming very pensive.

From all this it is obvious that I was still a complete child.

At times completely contradictory things happened. Occasionally, going to the office utterly repelled me: things reached the point where many times I went home feeling quite ill. Then suddenly, out of the blue, a bout of scepticism and indifference would set in (everything with me was in bouts) and then I would laugh at my own intolerance and squeamishness, and reproach myself with romanticism. I did not want to talk to anyone, but now I would go so far as to start a conversation with people and even consider striking up friendships with them. Suddenly, for no obvious reason, my fastidiousness would vanish at one stroke. Who knows, perhaps it had never even existed in me and was only assumed, borrowed from books? To this day I haven't solved this question. Once I even became great friends with them, started visiting their homes, playing preference, drinking vodka and discussing promotion . . . But please allow me to digress a little here.

Generally speaking, we Russians have never had in our ranks those stupid, starry-eyed romantics of the German variety, especially the French type who don't turn a hair at anything – even if the ground were to open up beneath them, even if the whole of France were perishing at the barricades they would still stay the same, they would not change, not even out of common decency, but would carry on singing their transcendental songs to their dying day, so to speak, because they are fools. But here, on Russian soil, we have no fools, that's a well-known fact; that's why we differ from other, Germanic, countries. Consequently, transcendental natures are not to be found among us in their pure form. It was our 'positive' publicists and critics of those days who, in pursuit of Kostanzhoglos and Uncle Pyotr Ivanoviches,[22] stupidly taking them as our ideal, invented all that stuff about our romantics, considering them just as other-worldly as in France or Germany. On the contrary – the characteristics of our romantics are the complete and diametrical opposite of the transcendental European variety and not one European criterion applies here. (Permit me to use this word 'romantic' – it is an ancient, venerable, time-honoured word and familiar to all.) The characteristics of our romantic type are: *to see everything and often to see it incomparably more clearly than our finest intellects*; not to be reconciled with anyone or anything, but at the same time not to baulk at anything; always evading difficulties; deferring to everyone and behaving tactfully to everyone; never losing sight of useful, practical goals (such as rent-free apartments, nice little pensions, or medals) and never forgetting those aims for all these enthusiasms and dainty volumes of lyrical verse, while at the same time preserving inviolate in himself to his dying day the 'sublime and beautiful' and appropriately preserving himself completely cocooned in cotton wool, like some piece of jewellery, ostensibly for the benefit of that very same 'sublime and beautiful'. Our romantic is a man of broad vision and the most accomplished of all our swindlers – I can assure you of that . . . even from personal experience. Of course, all this only applies if the romantic is clever. But what am I saying? The romantic is always clever and I merely wished to point out that even if we may have had our romantic fools they don't count, solely because when they were in their prime they were finally reborn as Germans, and to preserve their jewel more conveniently they settled somewhere over there, chiefly in Weimar or the Black Forest. I, for instance, genuinely despised my office job and it was only sheer necessity that prevented me from saying to hell with it, since all I did was sit there and get paid for it. Therefore – please note – I didn't say to hell with it. Our romantic would sooner go insane (which is very rare, however) but he doesn't give a damn if he has no other job in mind and he'll never be thrown out on his neck, although he might be hauled off to the madhouse because he thinks he's the 'King of Spain'[23] – and that's only if he really has gone stark raving mad. You see, only the anaemic and fair-haired go out of their minds in Russia. But we have an incalculable number of romantics and they subsequently attain exalted rank. Such astonishing versatility! And what capacity for the most contradictory sensations! Even at that time these thoughts comforted me and even now I hold the same views. That's why we have so many 'broad natures' who, even in their ultimate decline, never lose sight of their ideal. And though they may not lift a finger for that ideal, although they may be out-and-out thieves and gangsters, they still respect their original ideal to the point of tears and are uncommonly pure of heart. Oh yes, sir, it's only with us that the most inveterate scoundrel can be utterly and even sublimely pure of heart without at the same time ceasing to be a scoundrel in any way. I repeat, from among our romantics such businesslike rogues (I use the word 'rogue' with affection) emerge pretty often and they suddenly display such a feeling for reality, such practical awareness, that their astonished superiors and the public can only click their tongues at them in utter amazement.

This versatility is truly staggering and God only knows what it might turn into, how it will subsequently develop and what it holds in store for us in future. And the material isn't at all bad! I don't say this out of some sort of ridiculous or jingoistic patriotism. However, I'm convinced that again you're thinking that I'm trying to be funny. And who knows, perhaps the opposite's true, that is you're convinced that's what I really do think. At any rate, gentlemen, I shall consider either of your views as an honour and a particular pleasure. But please forgive this digression.

Of course, I didn't keep up my friendship with my colleagues; very soon I fell out with them and owing to my still youthful inexperience at the time even stopped greeting them, giving them the cold shoulder, as it were. However, this happened to me only once. In general I was always alone.

To begin with, at home I spent most of my time reading. I wanted to stifle all that was continuously boiling up inside me through external impressions. Out of all external impressions, reading was the only one possible for me. Of course, reading helped a lot – it excited, delighted and tormented me. But at times it bored me to death. For all that I still wanted to be doing things and I would suddenly plunge into dark, subterranean, vile, not so much depravity as petty dissipation. My mean, trivial, lusts were keen and fiery as a result of my constant, morbid irritability. The surges were hysterical, always accompanied by tears and convulsions. Apart from reading I had nowhere to turn – I mean, there was nothing in my surroundings that I could respect then or to which I might have been attracted. Moreover, dreadful ennui was seething within me, a hysterical craving for contradictions and contrasts would make its presence felt, and so I launched into debauchery. I haven't just told you all this simply to excuse myself – not at all . . . But no! I've lied! To justify myself is exactly what I wanted, that's why I'm just making this trifling observation for my own benefit, gentlemen. I don't want to lie. I've given you my word.

My debauchery was solitary, nocturnal, furtive, timorous and sordid, and it was accompanied by a feeling of shame that did not desert me at the most depraved moments, at such times even culminating in curses. Even in those days I carried my underground deep within me. I was terrified that I might somehow be seen, or meet someone, be recognized. I frequented various extremely shady places.

One night as I was passing some wretched tavern, through a brightly lit window I saw some gentlemen standing around a billiard table doing battle with their cues and then one of their company was thrown out of the window. Any other time this would have positively sickened me, but I envied the ejected gentleman so much that I even walked straight into the billiard room. 'Perhaps,' I told myself, 'I'll get into a fight and I'll be thrown out of the window too.'

I wasn't drunk, but what should I do? To what state of hysteria depression can sometimes reduce one! But nothing came of it.

As things turned out I was even incapable of jumping out of the window and I finally made my exit without having had a fight. From the start I was confronted by an officer.

I was standing by the billiard table, inadvertently blocking the way of this officer who wanted to get past. He took me by the shoulders in complete silence and without a word of warning or explanation shifted me from where I was standing to another place and then walked on, as if he hadn't even seen me. I would have forgiven him for beating me, but in no way could I forgive him for moving me from one place to another and completely failing to notice me.

The devil knows what I would have given then for a real, for a more correct quarrel – a more proper, a more *literary* one, so to say! They'd treated me like a fly. The officer was about six feet tall, and I was short and emaciated. However, it was within my power to start a quarrel. All I needed to do was protest and of course I would have been thrown out of the window. But I reconsidered and preferred to . . . withdraw from the scene with bitter feelings.

I left the tavern confused and distressed, went straight home, and the very next day I continued my petty debauchery even more timidly, feeling more downtrodden and despondent than ever before and with tears in my eyes, so it seemed, but for all that, I persevered. Don't imagine, however, that I shied away from that officer through cowardice. I've never been a coward at heart, although in fact I constantly behaved like one – but wait a little before you laugh, there's an explanation for this. I have an explanation for everything that concerns me, rest assured.

Oh, if only that officer had been the type to agree to a duel! But no, he was one of those gentlemen (alas, long vanished!) who preferred to take action with billiard cues or, like Gogol's Lieutenant Pirogov,[24] complain through the authorities. These gentlemen never fought duels and in any case would have considered a duel with the likes of me, a wretched civilian clerk, not the done thing at all; and, generally speaking, for them a duel was something unthinkable, free-thinking and very French, but they themselves were ready to dish out insults, especially if they happened to be six feet tall.

So now it was not cowardice that made me withdraw, but unbounded vanity. I was not scared of the height of six feet, nor that I might be painfully beaten and thrown out of the window; true, I had sufficient physical courage, but I lacked moral courage. I was afraid that everyone there, from that smart aleck of a marker to the last diseased, pimply, miserable greasy-collared clerk, would fail to understand and would ridicule me when I made my protest and addressed them in literary language. Because to this day it's impossible for us to discuss a point of honour – I don't actually mean honour, but point of honour (*point d'honneur*) in anything but literary language. In ordinary language 'points of honour' are never mentioned. I was perfectly convinced (this instinct for reality, despite all my romanticism!) that all of them would simply die laughing and that the officer wouldn't simply (that is, inoffensively) have laid into me, but would certainly have shoved me with his knee all around the billiard table and only then would he have taken pity and thrown me out of the window. Of course, I couldn't allow this wretched episode to end just like that. Afterwards I often met the officer in the street and I observed him very closely. Only, I can't say whether *he* recognized *me*. Most probably not – certain indications led me to this conclusion. But as for me, I . . . looked at him with anger and loathing, and so it went on – for several years! My anger grew and strengthened as the years passed. At first I started making discreet inquiries about this officer. This I found most difficult, as I didn't know a soul. But once someone hailed him in the street when I was following at a short distance, as if I were on a lead, and so I discovered his surname. Another time I followed him right up to his flat and for ten copecks learnt from the caretaker where he lived, on which floor, whether on his own or with someone, etc – in short, everything that could be learnt from a caretaker. One morning, although I had never engaged in literary activities, I suddenly hit on the idea of denouncing that officer by caricaturing him in a short story. I took great delight in writing that story. I exposed him, I even libelled him. At first I disguised his name in such a way that it was instantly recognizable, but later, on mature reflection, I changed it and sent it off to *Fatherland Notes*.[25] But in those days there was still no denunciatory literature and my story wasn't published. This I found deeply annoying. At times I simply choked with anger. Finally I decided to challenge my enemy to a duel. I composed a beautiful, charming letter, begging him to apologize; in the event of a refusal I hinted at a duel in fairly strong terms. The letter was written in such a way that if the officer had had the least inkling of the 'sublime and beautiful' then no doubt he would have come running to me to throw his arms around my neck and offer me his friendship. Oh, how wonderful that would have been! What a life we would have spent together, what a life! He would have protected me with his exalted rank; I would have ennobled him with my culture and . . . well, with my ideas all kinds of things – so many – would have been possible! But just imagine, two years had passed since he first insulted me and my challenge was nothing but a glaring anachronism, despite all the skilfulness of my letter in explaining and concealing the anachronism. But thank God (to this day I tearfully thank the Almighty) I didn't send the letter. It makes my blood run cold when I recall what might have happened had I sent it. And then suddenly . . . suddenly I took my revenge in the simplest, most incredibly ingenious way! All of a sudden the most brilliant idea dawned on me. Sometimes, on holidays, I used to knock around the Nevsky Prospekt,[26] strolling down the sunny side between three and four o'clock. I mean to say, I didn't stroll at all there – rather, I suffered innumerable torments, humiliations and attacks of spleen; but most probably that was necessary. I darted along between passers-by in the ugliest manner, like a minnow, constantly making way for generals, Horse Guards officers or hussars, or genteel ladies. At those moments I had sharp shooting pains in my heart and a burning sensation down my back at the very thought of the sorry state of my outfit and of the wretchedness and vulgarity of my small darting figure. This was the most excruciating agony, an uninterrupted, intolerable humiliation brought about by the thought which turned into the most palpable and unvarying feeling that I was a fly in the eyes of all those society people, a revolting, obscene fly – more intelligent and nobler than anyone else – that goes without saying – but a fly nonetheless, always giving in to others, humiliated by everyone and insulted by everyone. Why I had brought this torment on myself, why I had to go to Nevsky Prospekt I really don't know, but I was simply *drawn* there at every opportunity.

At that time I was already beginning to experience surges of those pleasures of which I've already spoken in my first chapter. After that incident with the officer I was drawn to Nevsky Prospekt more strongly than ever. It was there that I met him most often, there that I feasted my eyes on him. He too used to go there, mostly on holidays. Although he would step aside for generals and other high-ranking personages and also dart between them like a minnow, nobodies like me – and even those just a cut above me – were trampled on; he would bear right down on them as if there were simply empty space before him and under no circumstances would he give way. Looking at him I revelled in my own anger and . . . bitterly made way for him every time. It tormented me to think that not even in the street could I be on anything like an equal footing with him. 'Why is it invariably *you* who are first to make way?' I kept questioning myself in a mad fit of rage, sometimes waking up at two o'clock in the morning. 'Why is it always *you* and not him? There can't be a law about it, surely it's not written down anywhere? Why shouldn't there be a little give and take, as is normally the case when refined gentlemen meet in the street? So, he steps back halfway and you do the same and in that way you pass each other in mutual respect.' But that never happened and *I* was the one who always stepped aside and he didn't even notice that I was giving way. And then the most amazing idea suddenly dawned on me: what if we should meet and I . . . didn't step to one side? Deliberately not step aside, even if it meant colliding with him? What about that? This daring idea gradually so possessed me that it gave me no peace. I dreamt of it incessantly and horribly and I deliberately went to Nevsky Prospekt more often in order to get a clearer picture of how I would do it when the time came. I was ecstatic. More and more my plan came to strike me as both practicable and possible. 'Of course, I won't exactly give him a shove,' I thought, already mellowing in advance at the idea from sheer joy, 'I'll simply not make way, bump right into him, not too painfully, but shoulder to shoulder, strictly according to the rules of etiquette; I'll bump into him only as hard as he bumps into me.' At last my mind was completely made up. But the preparations took ages. The first thing I did when I put my plan into action was to make myself more presentable and take a little trouble over my clothes. 'Just in case there should be a public scandal (and there the public is highly refined: a countess promenades there, Prince D— promenades there – the whole of literature promenades there), I have to be dressed decently – that creates a good impression and in certain ways puts one at once on an equal footing in the eyes of high society.' With this in mind I asked for my salary in advance and bought myself black gloves and a respectable hat from Churkin's. Black gloves struck me as more impressive and *bon ton* than the lemon ones that first tempted me. 'The colour's too bright, it makes it look as if I want to show off', so I didn't take the lemon ones. Long before this I had a good shirt ready, with white bone studs, but the overcoat seriously delayed matters. In itself my overcoat wasn't all that bad and it did keep me warm. But it was wadded, with a racoon collar that was the height of servility. Whatever the cost, it had to be changed for a beaver one, the kind worn by army officers. To acquire one I started frequenting the Gostiny Dvor[27] and after several attempts settled on cheap German beaver. Although German beavers show signs of wear in no time and begin to look terribly shabby, when newly bought they are really quite decent. And, after all, I only needed it for the one occasion. I asked the price, but it was still too expensive. After profound deliberation I decided to sell my racoon collar. As for the rest of the money, which was a tidy sum for someone like me, I decided to try and borrow it from Anton Antonych Setochkin, my head of department, a rather withdrawn, but solid and worthy gentleman who never lent money to anyone but to whom I had been specially recommended when I first started work by the important personage who had appointed me to the post. I suffered agonies. To ask Anton Antonych for a loan struck me as monstrous and shameful, I even didn't sleep for two or three nights – in general I slept very little at the time and felt delirious; my heartbeats would become very faint or suddenly my heart would start racing, racing, racing! . . . At first Anton Antonych was taken aback, then he frowned, pondered the matter and in the end lent me the money, in return for a signed receipt which gave him the right to have the loan repaid out of my salary within a fortnight. So at last everything was ready. A fine beaver collar reigned in place of the filthy racoon and gradually I prepared for action. I couldn't come to an immediate decision without first thinking the thing had to be managed skilfully, step by step. But I confess that after repeated attempts I had even begun to despair: we'd never collide with each other – and that was that! Either I wasn't quite ready or determined enough – once we seemed on the point of colliding, but then I again gave way and he walked on without noticing me. I even prayed every time I approached him that God might strengthen my resolve. Once, after I had finally made my mind up, it only ended by my getting in his way, since at the very last moment, when I was only a few inches away, my courage failed me. He calmly walked right through me and I rolled to one side like a ball. That night I was again feverish and delirious. And then suddenly everything came to the happiest possible conclusion. The previous night I had finally decided not to persevere with an enterprise doomed to failure and to abandon it all as a lost cause; with this in mind I went for a stroll along Nevsky Prospekt for the last time, just to see how I would abandon it all as hopeless. Suddenly, about three paces from my enemy, I unexpectedly made up my mind, screwed up my eyes – and we collided squarely, shoulder to shoulder! I didn't yield one inch and I passed him – on an absolutely equal footing! He didn't even look round and pretended not to have noticed. But he was only pretending, of that I am certain. To this day I'm quite sure of that! Of course, I came off the worse, as he was the stronger; but that wasn't the point. The point was, I had achieved my purpose, upheld my dignity, hadn't yielded an inch, and had put myself on the same social footing as him in public. I went home feeling completely avenged. I was jubilant. I celebrated my triumph and sang Italian arias. Of course, I shan't describe what happened to me three days later. If you've read the first chapter of the *Notes from Underground* you can guess for yourselves. The officer was later posted somewhere else; I haven't set eyes on him for fourteen years. What's he doing now, my dear old chum? Who's he trampling on now?

II

But my spell of petty dissipation was coming to an end and I became heartily sick of it all. I had pangs of remorse, but I drove them away: I felt nauseated enough already. Gradually, however, I grew accustomed to this too. I grew accustomed to everything, that is, I didn't actually grow accustomed but somehow agreed of my own free will to grin and bear it. But I had a certain outlet which reconciled me to everything and this was to escape into all that was 'sublime and beautiful' – in my dreams, of course. I indulged in an orgy of dreaming. I dreamt for three months on end, huddled up in my little corner and, believe me, at those moments I bore no resemblance to that gentleman who, in his chicken-hearted confusion, had sewn a German beaver collar onto his overcoat. Suddenly I became a hero. I wouldn't even have allowed that six-foot officer to visit me then. I couldn't even visualize what he looked like then. What my dreams were about and how I could be satisfied with them is difficult to say now, but at the time they did satisfy me. Yes, even now I gain a certain degree of satisfaction from them. My dreams were especially sweet and powerful after a bout of dissipation, when they were accompanied by remorse and tears, by curses and rapture. There were moments of such positive ecstasy, of such happiness, that I swear I didn't feel even the slightest stirring of derision within me. Yes, there was faith, hope, love. But that's precisely the point – at that time I blindly believed that by some miracle, through some external circumstance, all this would suddenly open up, offering a wide prospect of appropriate activity – philanthropic, beautiful and, most important, ready-made (what kind of activity I never knew but, most important, it should be ready-made) and then I would suddenly step out into the wide world, to all intents and purposes mounted on a white steed and crowned with laurel. I couldn't imagine myself playing a secondary role and this was exactly why in reality I quite happily adopted the last. Either a hero or muck – there was nothing in between. And this was my undoing, since in the muck I consoled myself with the thought that at other times I was a hero, but a hero who was disguising himself in the muck. It's shameful, I thought, for an ordinary person to wallow in muck, but a hero is too exalted to dirty himself completely, so therefore I could wallow in it a little. Remarkably, these surges of the 'sublime and beautiful' came upon me during bouts of dissipation and precisely when I was plumbing the depths. They arrived just like that, in distinct pulses, as if to make their presence felt, but their appearance didn't put paid to my debauchery, however. On the contrary, they seemed to enliven it by way of contrast and came in just the right quantity needed to make a good sauce. In this case the sauce consisted of contradiction and suffering, of agonized introspection, and all these torments and pinpricks lent a certain piquancy, even a meaning, to my debauchery – in brief, they performed the function of a good sauce perfectly. None of this was even lacking in a certain profundity. Indeed, how could I have agreed to a simple, vulgar, immediate, clerkish debauchery and yet borne all that filth! What could there have been in it to attract me and lure me out into the streets at night? Oh no, sir, I had a decent loophole for everything . . .

But how much love, oh Lord, how much love I used to experience in those dreams of mine, in those escapes into all that was 'sublime and beautiful'! Although that love was pure fantasy, although in reality it could never be applied to anything human, there was such an abundance of that love that later on I never felt the need to project it on to anything: that really would have been a superfluous luxury! Everything, however, always ended extremely happily, in a lazy and intoxicating transition into art, that is, into beautiful, ready-made forms of existence, forcibly stolen from poets and novelists and adapted to every possible kind of use and requirement. For example, I triumph over everyone; of course, all have crumbled to nothing and are compelled willy-nilly to recognize all my perfections and I forgive them all; a famous poet and courtier, I fall in love; I inherit untold millions and immediately donate them to the human race and at once confess my vices to the whole nation, which of course are not simple vices, but incorporate an extraordinary amount of the 'sublime and beautiful', something in the Manfredian[28] style. Everybody weeps and kisses me (otherwise what insensitive brutes they would be!) and I set off barefoot and hungry to preach new ideas and to rout the reactionaries at Austerlitz.[29] Then they strike up a march, an amnesty is called and the Pope agrees to leave Rome for Brazil.[30] Next there's a ball for the whole of Italy at the Villa Borghese,[31] which is on Lake Como, since Lake Como has been transported to Rome specifically for the occasion. And then a scene in the bushes, etc – as if you didn't know! You'll say that it's vulgar and ignoble to parade all this in public now after personally confessing to so many raptures and tears. But why should it be ignoble? Surely you don't think that I'm ashamed of all this or that it's sillier than anything in your own lives, gentlemen? What's more, let me assure you that some of it wasn't at all badly staged by me . . . Not everything took place on Lake Como. But you're quite right; it really is vulgar and contemptible. But most contemptible of all is that I've started justifying myself to all of you. But even more contemptible than that is the fact that I'm making this observation now . . . Well, enough of this, or I'll never finish: one thing will be more contemptible than what came before it . . .

I was never capable of spending more than three months on end dreaming and I began to feel an irresistible need to plunge into society. For me, plunging into society meant going to visit my head of department, Anton Antonych Setochkin. He was the only regular acquaintance I had in my whole life, a circumstance that surprises me even now. But I only visited him during one of those bouts and my dreams reached such a peak of bliss that it was an absolute necessity to embrace people and all mankind immediately. To do that I needed to have at least one person at hand, someone who really existed. However, I could only visit Anton Antonych on Tuesdays (that was the day he received visitors), so therefore I had to postpone this need to embrace the whole of humanity until a Tuesday came along. This Anton Antonych lived at Five Corners,[32] in a third-floor flat with four low-ceilinged rooms, each smaller than the last, all very spartan and jaundiced-looking. He had two daughters – and there was an aunt, who used to pour out the tea. The daughters – one was thirteen, the other fourteen – had little snub noses and they always made me feel terribly embarrassed by their constant giggling and whispering. The host would usually sit in his study on a leather sofa in front of the table, together with some grey-haired guest, an official from our department or even from some other. I never saw more than two or three guests there, always the same. They would talk about excise duty, haggling in the Senate, salaries, promotion, His Excellency and how to get into his good books, etc, etc. I had the patience to sit next to these people like a complete idiot for four hours at a stretch, listening to them, neither daring to nor capable of discussing anything with them. I would sit there in a dull stupor and on several occasions I broke into a sweat, with a feeling of paralysis hanging over me. But all this was useful and good for me. When I returned home I would temporarily set aside my desire to embrace all mankind.

However, I apparently had another acquaintance, Simonov, an old school friend of mine. Very likely there were many of my former school-fellows in St Petersburg, but I didn't mix with them and even stopped greeting them in the street. Perhaps the reason for my moving to another government department was to distance myself from them and to cut myself off at one stroke from my loathsome boyhood. Curse that school and those terrible years of penal servitude! In short, I broke with my school-fellows the moment I regained my freedom. There remained just two or three whom I still greeted when I met them. One of them was Simonov, a very quiet and even-tempered person who hadn't distinguished himself in any way at school but in whom I discerned a certain independence of character and even integrity. I don't even think he was as limited as all that. Once we used to spend some fairly cheerful moments together, but they were short-lived and suddenly seemed to become shrouded in mist. Obviously he found these reminiscences oppressive and always appeared afraid that I might lapse into my former tone with him. I suspected that he found me extremely repulsive, but as I wasn't really certain of this I still visited him.

And then, one Thursday, unable to bear my solitude any longer and knowing that Anton Antonych's door would be closed on Thursdays, I remembered Simonov. As I climbed the stairs to his third-floor flat I was in fact thinking that this gentleman found my company disagreeable and that I was wasting my time going there. However, as it always came about that reflections of this kind only egged me on all the more, as if deliberately, to put myself in an ambiguous situation, I went in. It was almost a year since I had last seen Simonov.

III

I found two more of my school-fellows with him. They were evidently discussing something very important. Not one of them paid much attention to my arrival, which was rather odd, since

I hadn't seen them for years. Apparently they considered me some kind of common house-fly. Even at school I hadn't been treated like this, although all of them had hated me there. I realized, of course, that they were bound to despise me now because of my unsuccessful civil service career and because I had let myself go so badly and went around in scruffy clothes and so on – things that in their eyes proclaimed my ineptitude and mediocrity. All the same, I never expected such contempt. Simonov was even surprised when I arrived. Even before he had always seemed surprised whenever I turned up. All this puzzled me. Somewhat dejected, I sat down and started listening to their conversation.

A serious and even heated conversation was in progress about a farewell dinner that these gentlemen wanted to organize jointly the very next day for their friend Zverkov,[33] an army officer who had been posted to some remote part of the provinces. Monsieur Zverkov had been at school with me the whole time I was there. I grew to hate him, particularly in the upper forms. In the lower forms he was just a pretty, lively little chap whom everyone liked. I, however, loathed him even in the lower forms – just because he was such a pretty, lively little chap. He was consistently bad at lessons and the longer he was at the school the worse he got. But he passed his final exams because he was well connected. In his last year there he was left an estate of two hundred serfs and since most of us were poor he started bragging about it to us. He was vulgar in the highest degree, but for all that a decent fellow, even when he was bragging. Despite our superficial, far-fetched and stereotyped formulae of honour, all of us, with very few exceptions, toadied to Zverkov the more he boasted. And we didn't ingratiate ourselves in the hope of gaining something by it, but because he was a person blessed with the gifts of nature. Besides, it had somehow become accepted among us to consider Zverkov an expert in the department of social skills and good manners. The latter particularly infuriated me. I hated the piercing, cocksure sound of his voice, the way he adored his own witticisms which invariably came across as extremely silly, although he did have a very sharp tongue. I hated his handsome but stupid face (for which, however, I would willingly have exchanged my *intelligent* one) and those casual forties-style officer's manners. I hated the fact that he talked of his *future* successes with women (he had decided not to start womanizing until he received his officer's epaulettes, which he was impatiently awaiting) and said that he would be fighting duels non-stop. I remember how once, although I was always the silent type, I suddenly came to grips with Zverkov when he was chatting with his friends in a free period about his forthcoming amours and finally growing as playful as a puppy in the sunshine, he suddenly announced that not one of the peasant girls on his estate would escape his attentions, that this was his *droit de seigneur*,[34] and that if the peasants so much as protested he'd have the lot of them flogged and would double that bearded rabble's rent. Our louts applauded him, while I argued with him – not because I felt at all sorry for the girls and their fathers, but simply because they were applauding an insect like him. On that occasion I won the day, but although Zverkov was a fool, he was cheerful and cheeky and laughed the whole thing off so well, that in fact I didn't really win at all: the laugh was on his side. After that he got the better of me several times, but without any malice, jokingly as it were, casually, laughing. I was too angry and contemptuous to offer a rejoinder. After we left school he made overtures to me; I offered little resistance, I was so flattered, but we quickly and naturally went our own ways. Later I heard of his success as a barrack-room lieutenant and of his *boozing*. Then other rumours circulated about how he was *succeeding* in the army. No longer did he greet me in the street and I suspected he was afraid of compromising himself by exchanging greetings with a nobody like me. Once I spotted him in the theatre, in the third row of the circle, already sporting aiguillettes. He was bowing and scraping, and making up to the daughters of some very ancient general. In three years he had gone terribly to seed, although he was still quite handsome and sprightly. He had a somewhat bloated look and had put on weight. Obviously, by the time he was thirty, he'd be really flabby. It was in honour of this same finally departing Zverkov that our friends wanted to give a dinner. They had hung around with him for the entire three years, although in their heart of hearts they didn't consider themselves his equal – of that I am convinced.

Of Simonov's two guests one was a Russo-German, Ferfichkin, a short fellow with an ape-like face, a perfect idiot who poked fun at everyone and who had been my bitterest enemy ever since the lowest forms – an odious, insolent show-off, posing as someone of the most refined arrogance, although he was of course a rotten coward at heart. He was among those admirers of Zverkov who played up to him from ulterior motives and often borrowed money from him. Simonov's other guest, Trudolyubov, was an unremarkable character – the military type, tall, with a chilly air, fairly honest but one who worshipped success of any kind and who was incapable of discussing anything except promotion. Apparently he happened to be a distant relative of Zverkov's and this, stupidly enough, gave him a certain status among us. He always considered me a nonentity; but he treated me if not altogether politely at least tolerably.

'All right,' said Trudolyubov, 'if it's seven roubles each and there's three of us – that makes twenty-one roubles and for that we can dine jolly well. Of course, Zverkov won't be paying.'

'Of course not, if we're inviting him!' Simonov said decisively.

'Do you really think,' Ferfichkin cut in haughtily, with the fervour of an insolent lackey boasting of his master the general's decorations, 'do you really suppose that Zverkov will allow us to foot the whole bill? He'll accept out of tactfulness, but then he'll stand us a half-dozen bottles.'

'But what are the four of us going to do with a half-dozen bottles?' observed Trudolyubov, concerned only with the half-dozen.

'Well then, three of us – four with Zverkov – that's twenty-one roubles – at the Hôtel de Paris, tomorrow at five o'clock,' concluded Simonov, who had been chosen to organize proceedings.

'But how do you arrive at twenty-one?' I said with some agitation, making myself out to be rather offended. 'If you include me it makes twenty-eight, not twenty-one.'

I felt that my sudden and totally unexpected offer would

strike them as a handsome gesture and that they would all be won over and look upon me with respect.

'Surely *you* don't want to come too, do you?' Simonov replied in annoyance, somehow avoiding eye contact with me. He knew me through and through.

I was furious that he knew me through and through.

'Why not? After all, I was at school with him as well. I must confess I'm rather hurt at being left out,' I spluttered again.

'And where were we supposed to look for you?' Ferfichkin rudely put in.

'You never hit it off with Zverkov,' added Trudolyubov, frowning. But now I had seized on the idea I wouldn't let go . . .

'It strikes me that no one has the right to judge that,' I retorted with trembling voice, as if God knows what had happened. 'Perhaps it's precisely because we didn't hit it off that I want to come now.'

'Who the hell can make you out? . . . All these lofty sentiments . . .' Trudolyubov sniggered.

'We'll put your name down,' decided Simonov, turning to me. 'Tomorrow at five o'clock, at the Hôtel de Paris. Don't get it wrong.'

'What about the money?' Ferfichkin said in a low voice to Simonov, nodding towards me, but he stopped short, since even Simonov was embarrassed.

'All right,' said Trudolyubov, 'if he wants to come so badly then let him.'

'But really, we're just an intimate little circle of friends,' fumed Ferfichkin as he picked up his hat. 'It's not an official gathering. Perhaps we don't want you to come at all . . .'

They left. Ferfichkin did not even bow to me as he went and Trudolyubov nodded slightly, without looking at me. Simonov, with whom I was now left face to face, appeared to be in a state of vexed bewilderment and gave me an odd look. He did not sit down, nor did he invite me to.

'Hmm . . . yes . . . so, it's tomorrow. Are you going to hand over the money now? I'm asking, as I'd like to know for certain . . .' he muttered, with an embarrassed look.

I flared up but as I did so I remembered that from time

immemorial I'd owed Simonov fifteen roubles and although I'd never forgotten them, I'd never paid them back either.

'You yourself must agree, Simonov, I couldn't have known when I came here . . . and I'm very upset that I forgot . . .'

'All right, all right, it doesn't matter. Pay me tomorrow at the dinner. I only wanted to know . . . Now please don't . . .'

He stopped short and started pacing the room with even greater annoyance. As he did this he came down on his heels, stamping all the harder.

'I'm not keeping you, am I?' I asked after a two-minute silence.

'Oh no,' he replied with a start. 'Well, to be honest . . . yes . . . You see, I've got to drop in somewhere . . . not very far from here . . .' he added rather apologetically and somewhat ashamed.

'Good Lord! Why on earth didn't you say so?' I cried, grabbing my peaked cap in a surprised but nonchalant manner, which came from God knows where.

'It's not far at all . . . just a couple of steps . . .' Simonov repeated, seeing me to the front door with a busy look, which did not suit him at all.

'So, tomorrow at five o'clock sharp!' he shouted down the stairs. He was truly delighted that I was leaving. But I was absolutely fuming.

'Whatever possessed me, whatever made me put myself forward?' I said to myself, gnashing my teeth as I strode along the street. And as for that rotten swine Zverkov! Of course, I shouldn't really go; of course, I should say to hell with it. I don't have to go, do I? I'll send them a note in the post tomorrow . . .'

But what so infuriated me was that I knew very well that I would go; that I would go on purpose; and that the more tactless, the more inappropriate it was to go, the more certain it was that I would go.

And there was even one positive obstacle to my going: I didn't have the money. All I had in the world was nine roubles. But out of that I had to pay seven to my servant Apollon, who lived with me, as his month's wages, without keep.

Given Apollon's character, not to pay him was out of the question. But more about that swine, that thorn in my flesh, later.

However, I knew that I wouldn't pay him all the same and that I would definitely go.

That night I had the most terrible nightmares. And no wonder: the whole evening I was oppressed by memories of those miserable years of penal servitude at school and I couldn't shake them off. I had been dumped at that school by some distant relatives on whom I depended and of whom I've since heard nothing. I was sent there as an orphan, already crushed by their reproaches, already introspective, silent and looking at everything around me like a savage. My school-fellows greeted me with spiteful and merciless sneers because I wasn't like any of them. But I couldn't bear those sneers, I couldn't get on with them as easily as they got on with each other. I conceived an immediate loathing for them and sought refuge in my timorous, wounded but excessive pride. Their uncouthness deeply disturbed me. They laughed cynically at my face, at my clumsy figure – yet how stupid their own faces were! In our school facial expressions tended to become particularly stupid and degenerate. So many handsome boys entered the school but within a few years it simply revolted you to look at them. By the time I was sixteen I looked upon them in sullen amazement; even then I was startled by the triviality of their ideas, the stupidity of their pursuits, their games, their conversations. They had little understanding of what really mattered, took so little interest in the most stimulating, inspiring subjects that I couldn't help considering them my inferiors. It wasn't wounded vanity that drove me to that and for God's sake don't try and get at me with such sickeningly banal retorts as: 'I was only dreaming, whereas they understood real life.'

They understood nothing, nothing of real life, and I swear it was this that exasperated me most about them. On the contrary, their conception of the most strikingly obvious reality was fantastically stupid and even then they were used to worshipping nothing but success. Everything that was just, but downtrodden and oppressed, they mocked callously and disgracefully. They took rank for intelligence; at sixteen they were already discussing cushy little jobs. Of course, much of this could be blamed on the stupidity and bad examples that were the constant companions of their childhood and adolescence. They were monstrously depraved. Of course, this was more of a façade, more affected cynicism; of course, youth, and a certain freshness could be glimpsed in them despite their depravity. But in them even the freshness was unappealing and manifested itself in a kind of rakishness. I hated them intensely, although I was perhaps even worse than they were. They repaid me in kind and made no attempt to conceal their loathing for me. But I no longer wanted them to like me; on the contrary, I constantly longed for their humiliation. To escape their sneers I deliberately began to study as hard as I could and soon advanced to the top of the class. That did impress them. Moreover, they were all gradually coming to realize that I was already reading books that were well beyond them and understood things (not part of our special curriculum) of which they had never even heard. They looked on all this with wild mockery, but they were morally subservient, all the more so since in this respect even the teachers paid attention to me. The sneers ceased, but the hostility remained and from now on cold, strained relations were established. In the end I myself couldn't hold out any longer: with the passing years I developed the need for people, for friends. I tried to get close to a few of them, but this attempted rapprochement always turned out unnatural and so it simply fizzled out of its own accord. I did once have a friend. But I was already a despot at heart, I wanted to have unlimited authority over his soul; I wanted to instil in him a contempt for his surroundings; I demanded that he should make an arrogant and definitive break with those surroundings. I frightened him with my passionate friendship, I reduced him to tears, to nervous convulsions. He was a naive, submissive soul, but when he surrendered himself completely to me I immediately hated him and brushed him aside – it was just as if I'd needed him only to win victory over him, simply to bring about his total submission. But I couldn't get the better of everyone. My friend was also quite unlike any of the others and in this he was an extremely rare exception. The first thing I did on leaving school was to abandon the special career for which I was earmarked in order to sever all ties, cursing the past and scattering it to the winds . . . The devil only knows what made me drag myself off to Simonov's after that! . . .

Early next morning I leapt out of bed feeling terribly excited, as if everything would come to fruition right away. I believed that some radical turning-point in my life was approaching and was bound to come that very day. Whether it was through lack of experience, perhaps, but all my life it had struck me that whenever any external event occurred, even the most trivial, some radical change in my life would immediately take place. However, I went to the office as usual, but slipped away two hours early to get ready. The important thing, so I thought, was not to arrive first or they might think I was only too delighted to be going to the dinner. But there were thousands of important things like this and all of them worried me into a state of impotence. I polished my boots again myself: nothing in the world would have induced Apollon to polish them twice a day – that would have been quite out of order. So I cleaned them myself, sneaking the brushes from the hall so that he couldn't see me and despise me for it later. Then I gave my clothes a close inspection and found that everything was old, worn out, threadbare: I'd really become terribly slovenly. However, my office uniform was fairly presentable, but I simply couldn't go out to dinner in my uniform! The main problem was the huge yellow spot right on the trouser knee. I anticipated that this spot alone would deprive me of nine-tenths of my personal dignity. I knew that it was very low of me to think like that. 'But now's not the time for thinking, now reality is approaching!' I thought – and at that my spirits drooped. I also knew very well even then that I was monstrously exaggerating all these facts, but what could I do? I was no longer in control of myself and I was shaking feverishly. In my despair I visualized how patronizingly and icily that 'scoundrel' Zverkov would greet me; with what stupid, positively invincible contempt that blockhead Trudolyubov would look at me; how nastily and insolently that louse Ferfichkin would sneer at my expense, just to worm his way into Zverkov's favour; how perfectly Simonov would understand all this and despise me for the meanness of my vanity and my faint-heartedness; and, most of all, how sordid, how *unliterary*, how pedestrian it would all be. Of course, the best thing was not to go at all. But this was more impossible than anything: once I had got the idea in my head I was totally committed. For the rest of my life I would have taunted myself: 'You got cold feet, you were frightened of *reality* – yes, you got cold feet!' But no, I dearly wanted to show that 'riff-raff' that I wasn't such a coward as I myself imagined. What's more, in my most violent paroxysm of feverish cowardice I still dreamed of gaining the upper hand, making mincemeat of them, winning them over, forcing them to like me – well, if only for the 'loftiness of my thoughts and undeniable wit'. They would desert Zverkov and he would take a back seat, silent and ashamed, and I would crush him. Later, perhaps, I might make it up with him and drink with him as an intimate friend; but the most galling and most hurtful thing for me was that even then – I knew this without any shadow of doubt – in actual fact, I needed none of this and that, in actual fact, I didn't have the slightest inclination to crush, subjugate or attract them and that even if I were to achieve all that I myself would be the first not to give a damn for the outcome. Oh, how I prayed for that day to be over quickly! In inexpressible anguish I went over to the window, opened the hinged pane and peered out into the murky dimness of the thickly falling wet snow . . .

Finally my shoddy wall clock wheezed five o'clock. I grabbed my hat and, trying not to look at Apollon who had been waiting for me to hand over his wages since morning but was too proud to broach the matter first, slipped past him through the door and in a smart cab that I had specially hired with my last fifty copecks, I bowled along like a lord to the Hôtel de Paris.

IV

I already knew since the previous evening that I'd be first to arrive. But it wasn't a matter of who arrived first.

Not only was no one there, but I even had difficulty finding our room. The table wasn't fully laid yet. What could that mean? After much questioning I finally ascertained from the waiters that dinner had been ordered for six o'clock, not for five. This was confirmed in the bar. I even felt ashamed that I had to ask. It was still only twenty-five past five. If they had changed the time then they should at least have informed me – that was what the post was for – and not subjected me to this 'indignity', both in my own eyes and in front of the waiters. I sat down; a waiter started laying the table. Somehow I felt even more humiliated in his presence. Towards six o'clock candles were brought in, in addition to the lamps that were already lit – the waiter hadn't thought of bringing them immediately I arrived. In the next room two gloomy, angry-looking hotel guests were dining in silence at separate tables. From one of the rooms furthest away came a dreadful racket. There was even shouting and I could hear the loud guffaws of a whole gang of people and some foul, French-sounding shrieks: there were ladies dining there too. In short, it was all truly sickening. Rarely have I lived through worse moments, so that when they all arrived at exactly six o'clock I was initially so delighted to see them, as if they were my liberators, that I almost forgot that I was supposed to look offended.

Zverkov entered at the head of them – obviously he was the leader. He and all the others were laughing, but on seeing me Zverkov assumed a dignified air, came over to me without hurrying himself, bending slightly forward from the waist as if to show off and offering his hand – amiably but not too familiarly – with the somewhat guarded courtesy of a general, as if by doing so he was protecting himself from something. I had imagined that, on the contrary, the moment he entered he would have laughed that shrill, high-pitched laugh of his right from the start and immediately produced those weak jokes and witticisms of his. I had been preparing myself for them from the day before, but I hadn't in the least expected such condescending, such overbearing affability. So, now he considered himself immeasurably superior to me in every respect. If he had only wanted to insult me by behaving like a general that wouldn't have mattered, I thought. One way or the other I would have shrugged it off. But what if, in actual fact, without any wish to cause offence, he had seriously got the idea in his stupid mutton-head that he was immeasurably superior to me and that the only way he could possibly treat me was patronizingly? This assumption alone made me choke with anger.

'It came to me as a surprise when I learnt of your desire to join us,' he began, lisping affectedly, drawling and mouthing his words in a way he never used to. 'Somehow we never seem to meet. You fight shy of us. There's no need to. We're not so frightening as you think. In any event I'm pleased to re-ne-ew . . .'

And he turned away nonchalantly to put his hat on the window sill.

'Have you been waiting long?' asked Trudolyubov.

'I arrived at five sharp, as I was told to yesterday,' I replied in a loud voice, with irritation that threatened an imminent explosion.

'Surely you must have told him we changed the time?' asked Trudolyubov, turning to Simonov.

'I didn't – I forgot,' he replied and, without a trace of remorse, and without even a word of apology, he went off to see about the hors d'œuvre.

'So, you've been here an hour already – oh, you poor chap!' Zverkov exclaimed sarcastically, since in his opinion the whole thing was really terribly funny. And after him that rotter Ferfichkin broke into his nasty high-pitched laughter that sounded like a wretched little dog squealing. He too found my situation amusing and embarrassing.

'It's not in the least funny!' I shouted at Ferfichkin, growing increasingly incensed. 'It's the others' fault, not mine. No one bothered to tell me. It's . . . it's . . . it's simply absurd!'

'Not only absurd, but more than that,' Trudolyubov muttered, naively standing up for me. 'That's putting it too mildly! It's downright rude! Of course, it wasn't intentional. But how could Simonov have . . . hm!'

'If someone had treated me like that,' observed Ferfichkin, 'I'd have . . .'

'But you could have ordered a little something in the meantime,' interrupted Zverkov, 'or simply dined without waiting for us . . .'

'You'll agree that I didn't need anyone's permission for that,' I snapped. 'If I waited it was because . . .'

'Come on, let's sit down, gentlemen,' cried Simonov as he came back. 'Everything's ready and I can vouch that the champagne's beautifully chilled . . . You see, I didn't have your address, so where was I supposed to find you?' he said, suddenly turning to me but again avoiding eye contact. Clearly he had something against me. He must have had second thoughts after yesterday.

Everyone sat down and I followed suit. The table was a round one. On my left I had Trudolyubov, with Simonov on my right. Zverkov was sitting opposite, with Ferfichkin next to him, between him and Trudolyubov.

'Now, ple-ea-se te-tell me . . . do you work in a government department?' Zverkov continued, still giving me his attention. When he saw that I was upset he seriously imagined that I should be shown some kindness, that I needed to be cheered up, so to speak. 'What does he want? Does he want me to chuck a bottle at him?' I thought, in a terrible rage. Not being used to this sort of thing I grew excited unnaturally quickly.

'In a certain office,' I replied brusquely, peering at my plate.

'And do y-you f-find it r-r-remuner-rative? Tell me, what ind-d-duced you to leave your previous job?'

'What ind-d-duced me was that I just w-w-anted to l-leave my previous j-j-job,' I drawled three times as much as him, barely able to control myself. Ferfichkin snorted. Simonov glanced at me ironically; Trudolyubov stopped eating and began looking me over quizzically. Zverkov winced, but pretended not to notice.

'We-well now, what's your p-pay?'

'My pay?'

'I mean – your s-salary?'

'Why this cross-examination?'

However, I immediately told him what my salary was and flushed crimson.

'That's nothing much,' Zverkov observed pompously.

'Oh no, you can't dine in smart restaurants on that!' Ferfichkin added insolently.

'In my opinion it's a mere pittance,' Trudolyubov remarked gravely.

'And how thin you've grown, how you've changed . . . since those days,' added Zverkov, not without venom, eyeing me and my clothes with brazen pity.

'Now stop embarrassing him,' tittered Ferfichkin.

'My dear sir, I'll have you know that I'm not in the least embarrassed,' I finally blurted out. 'Do you hear? I'm dining here, in this "smart restaurant", at my own, at my *own* expense and not at other people's. Please take note, Monsieur Ferfichkin.'

'Wha-at!? Which one of us here isn't dining at his own expense? It seems you . . .' Ferfichkin latched on, turning red as a lobster and looking me frenziedly in the eye.

'Well now,' I replied, feeling I'd gone a bit too far. 'I suggest we have a rather more intelligent conversation.'

'It seems you're determined to demonstrate your intelligence!'

'Don't worry, it would be really wasted here.'

'What on earth are you ca-ca-cackling about, my dear sir, eh? You haven't gone off your r-rocker in your *l*epartment, have you?'

'Enough, gentlemen, enough!' Zverkov cried imperiously.

'This is all so silly! Here we are, gathered together as good friends to wish a dear comrade bon voyage,' observed Trudolyubov, rudely addressing me alone, 'and you're counting the cost. It was you who thrust yourself on us yesterday, so don't go upsetting the general harmony . . .'

'That's enough, enough,' exclaimed Zverkov. 'Stop it, gentlemen, this won't do at all. You'd better let me tell you how I nearly got married the day before yesterday . . .'

And he embarked on some scandalous story about how he had nearly got married two days before. However, there wasn't a word about a marriage and the narrative was peopled with generals and colonels and even gentlemen of the bedchamber, with Zverkov almost the leading light. There followed bursts of approving laughter; Ferfichkin positively yelped.

They all abandoned me and I sat there, crushed and humiliated.

'Heavens! Is this my kind of company?' I thought. 'And what a laughing-stock I've made of myself in front of them! All the same, I let Ferfichkin get away with murder. Those boobies honestly think they've done me an honour by giving me a place at their table, but they don't seem to understand that it's me, it's *me*, who's doing *them* the honour and not the other way round. "You've got thinner! That suit!" Oh, damn those trousers! Zverkov must have noticed the yellow spot on the knee just now . . . Well, what of it . . . ? I should really get up now, this instant, take my hat and simply leave, without a word . . . Out of contempt! Even if it means a duel tomorrow. The bastards! As if I grudged a measly seven roubles. But perhaps they'll think . . . Oh, what the hell! I don't grudge seven roubles! I'm going this instant . . . !'

Needless to say, I stayed.

I drowned my misery in Château Lafite and sherry by the glassful. Being unused to drink, I very soon got tipsy and the more I drank the more incensed I became. Suddenly I felt the urge to insult the lot of them in the most audacious manner and then make my departure. Just seize the right moment and show them who they're dealing with – then they could at least say: he may be ridiculous but he's very intelligent . . . and . . . and . . . in short, to hell with them!

Insolently, I looked them all over with glazed eyes. But it seemed they had completely forgotten about me. *They* were noisy, boisterous, cheerful. Zverkov did all the talking. I listened hard. He was telling them about some ravishing lady whom he had finally brought to the point of declaring her love for him (naturally, he was lying like a trooper) and how he had been greatly assisted in this affair by a bosom pal, a certain princeling called Kolya, an officer of the Hussars, who owned three thousand serfs.

'And yet this Kolya with the three thousand serfs is obviously not here to see you off,' I said, suddenly breaking into the conversation. For a moment no one said a word.

'You're drunk already,' Trudolyubov said, at last deigning to acknowledge my presence and casting a contemptuous glance in my direction. Zverkov was silently eyeing me as if I were some nasty insect. I looked down. Simonov hurriedly started pouring the champagne.

Trudolyubov raised his glass and everyone except me followed suit.

'Your very good health and a prosperous journey!' he shouted to Zverkov. 'To old times, gentlemen, and to the future. Hurrah!'

Everyone drained his glass and went over to embrace Zverkov. I didn't budge. My full glass was standing in front of me, untouched.

'Surely you're going to drink his health?' bellowed Trudolyubov, losing patience and turning towards me menacingly.

'I wish to make a speech of my own, separately . . . and then I'll drink, Mr Trudolyubov.'

'Bad-tempered brute!' growled Simonov.

I drew myself up in my chair and feverishly clutched my glass, preparing myself to say something out of the ordinary, although I didn't have any idea what it would be.

'Silence!' shouted Ferfichkin. 'I'm sure we're going to hear something intelligent!'

Realizing what was going on, Zverkov waited very gravely.

'My dear Lieutenant Zverkov,' I began, 'I'd have you know that I detest big talk, phrase-mongers and tight waists . . . That's point number one and the second follows on from that . . .'

Everyone stirred uneasily.

'Point number two: I hate smutty stories and those who tell them. Especially those who tell them!'

'Point number three: I love truth, sincerity and honesty,' I continued almost mechanically as I was starting to freeze with terror and I didn't understand how I could be saying all this . . . 'I love ideas, Monsieur Zverkov. I love true comradeship, on an equal footing and not . . . hm . . . I love . . . But what's the point? I'll drink your health, too, Monsieur Zverkov. Now go and seduce all those Circassian maidens, shoot the enemies of the fatherland . . . and . . . and . . . your health, Monsieur Zverkov!'

Zverkov got up from the table, bowed and said: 'I'm really most obliged to you.'

He was terribly insulted and even turned pale.

'To hell with you!' roared Trudolyubov, banging his fist on the table.

'Oh yes, sir, people get punched in the mug for that!' shrieked Ferfichkin.

'He should be thrown out,' muttered Simonov.

'Not another word, gentlemen, don't do anything!' Zverkov solemnly shouted, putting a stop to the general indignation. 'I thank you all, but I myself am quite capable of showing him how much I value his words.'

'Mr Ferfichkin,' I said in a loud voice, imperiously turning to Ferfichkin. 'Tomorrow you will give me satisfaction for what you've just said.'

'You mean a duel, sir? With pleasure,' he replied. However, I really must have cut such a comical figure challenging him, it was so at odds with my diminutive stature, that everyone simply collapsed with laughter, Ferfichkin last of all.

'Yes, of course, chuck him out! He's obviously dead drunk!' Trudolyubov said with loathing.

'I'll never forgive myself for including him,' Simonov growled once more.

'Right now I'd like to throw a bottle at the lot of them,' I thought and I picked one up . . . and filled my glass to the brim. 'No . . . I'd better sit it out to the bitter end!' I thought.

'You'd be only too delighted if I left, gentlemen. Fat chance of that. I'll deliberately sit here and drink right to the end to show that I don't consider you of the slightest importance. I shall sit and drink because this is a low-class dive and I paid good money to come in. I shall sit here and drink, because I think you're a lot of nobodies – non-existent nobodies. I shall sit here and drink . . . and sing if I want to . . . yes . . . I'll sing, because I have the right to . . . sing . . . hmm.'

But I didn't sing. I merely tried to avoid looking at any of them; I adopted the most detached air and waited impatiently for them to speak first. But alas, they did not speak. And how I longed, how I longed to make it up with them at that moment! It struck eight and finally nine. They moved from the table to the divan. Zverkov stretched out on the sofa, resting one leg on a small round table. They took their wine with them. Zverkov did in fact contribute three bottles of his own. Of course, he didn't invite me. They all gathered around him on the divan, listening to him almost reverentially. Obviously they were very fond of him. 'Why? Why?' I wondered. Now and then they went into drunken raptures and embraced each other. They spoke of the Caucasus, the nature of true passion, the most advantageous postings in the army, how much a certain Hussar officer, Podkharzhevsky (whom none of them knew personally) earned and were delighted that he had such a large income; about the exceptional grace and beauty of Princess D—, whom none of them had ever set eyes on either; and finally they came to the conclusion that Shakespeare was immortal.

I smiled contemptuously and walked along the wall on the other side of the room, directly opposite the sofa, back and forth, from table to stove. I was trying my hardest to show them that I could do without them; at the same time I deliberately stamped on the floor, coming down hard on my heels. But it was all in vain. *They* took no notice whatsoever. I had the patience to keep walking up and down like that, right in front of them, from eight to eleven o'clock, always keeping to the same line from table to stove and back again. 'So, I'm walking because I want to and no one can forbid me.' A waiter stopped several times to look at me whenever he entered the room; the frequent turns made me feel giddy and at times I thought I was delirious. During those three hours I became soaked in sweat and three times I dried out again. At times the thought flashed through my mind and pierced my heart with the most excruciating pain that ten, twenty, forty years might pass and

I would still – even after forty years – recall with revulsion and humiliation these nastiest, most ridiculous and ghastliest moments of my whole life. To humiliate myself more shamefully and voluntarily was impossible – this I fully, all too fully, understood – yet still I continued my pacing from table to stove and back. 'Oh, if you only knew what feelings and thoughts I'm capable of and how cultured I am!' I thought at times, mentally addressing the divan on which my enemies were seated. But my enemies were behaving as if I wasn't even in the room. Once, only once, did they turn towards me – to be exact, just as Zverkov started holding forth about Shakespeare and I suddenly broke into contemptuous laughter. I gave vent to such artificial, revolting snorts that they all broke off their conversation at once and for about two minutes – gravely and without laughing – watched me as I walked along the wall, from table to stove, *without paying them the least attention*. But nothing happened: they said nothing and within two minutes had again deserted me. It struck eleven.

'Gentlemen!' cried Zverkov, rising from the divan. 'Let's all go *there* – now!'

'Of course, of course!' exclaimed the others.

I turned sharply towards Zverkov. I was so exhausted, so shattered that I felt like ending it all, even if it meant cutting my throat! I was feverish . . . My sweat-soaked hair stuck to my forehead and temples.

'Zverkov! I ask you for forgiveness!' I said brusquely and determinedly. 'And yours too, Ferfichkin – everyone's, everyone's. I've insulted everyone!'

'Aha! So duels aren't your cup of tea, eh?' Ferfichkin hissed venomously.

I felt a sharp stab of pain in my heart. 'Oh no, duels don't scare me, Ferfichkin! I'm ready to fight you tomorrow, even after a reconciliation. I insist on it and you cannot refuse. I want to show you that I'm not afraid of duels. You'll fire first and I'll fire into the air.'

'Likes his little joke!' observed Simonov.

'A load of hogwash!' retorted Trudolyubov.

'Now please allow me to pass, you're in my way! . . . Well,

what is it you want?' Zverkov replied contemptuously. All of them were red-faced and their eyes were shining: they'd had a great deal to drink.

'I'm asking for your friendship, Zverkov. I offended you, but . . .'

'Offended me? Y-you!? Offended *m-me*?! I'll have you know, my dear sir, that never, not under any circumstances, could you ever offend *me*!'

'We've just about had enough of you, so clear out!' said Trudolyubov, rounding things off. 'Let's go.'

'Olympia's all mine, gentlemen. Agreed?' shouted Zverkov.

'We won't argue!' they replied, laughing.

I stood there, totally rebuffed. The gang left the room noisily, Trudolyubov striking up some stupid song. Simonov stayed behind for a brief moment to tip the waiters. Suddenly I went up to him.

'Simonov! Lend me six roubles!' I said resolutely and desperately.

He looked at me in absolute amazement with his bleary eyes. He too was drunk. 'You don't mean to say you're coming *there* with us?'

'Oh yes!'

'I don't have any money!' he snapped, grinning disdainfully and sweeping out of the room.

I grabbed him by his overcoat: it was a nightmare. 'Simonov! I saw you had money, so why do you refuse? And am I really such a scoundrel? Now, mind you don't refuse me: if only you knew, if only you knew why I'm asking! Everything depends on it, my entire future, all my plans . . .'

Simonov took out some money and virtually hurled it at me.

'Take it, if you're so shameless!' he said mercilessly and ran off to catch up with the others.

For a minute I was left on my own. Disorder, leftovers, a broken glass on the floor, spilt wine, cigarette ends, intoxication and wild gibberish in my head, tormenting anguish in my heart – and finally that all-seeing, all-hearing waiter staring me curiously in the eye.

'*There!*' I yelled. 'Either they'll all go down on their knees, clasp my legs and beg for my friendship . . . or I'll give Zverkov a slap in the face!'

V

'So, here it is, here it is at last, that collision with reality,' I muttered, rushing headlong down the stairs. 'This, of course, is no longer the Pope leaving Rome and travelling to Brazil, it's obviously not a ball on Lake Como!'

'You're a scoundrel,' ran through my mind, 'if you can laugh at this now.'

'Oh, what the hell!' I shouted, answering myself. 'It's all over anyway!' There was no sign of them, but that didn't matter: I knew where they'd gone.

By the steps stood a solitary night cabby, his coarse peasant greatcoat completely powdered with snow that was still falling in wet, seemingly warm flakes. It was steamy and close outside. His shaggy little skewbald horse was also powdered with snow and was coughing – that I remember very clearly. I rushed to the sledge, but no sooner had I raised one foot to step in when the recollection of the way Simonov had given me those six roubles was the last straw and I slumped into it like a sack . . .

'No, I'll have to do a lot to redeem all this!' I shouted. 'But I shall redeem it, or I'll perish on the spot, this very night. Drive on!'

We moved off. A whole whirlwind was raging in my head.

'Going down on their knees to beg for my friendship – that they won't do! That's a mirage, a vulgar mirage, disgusting, romantic, fantastic, just like the ball on Lake Como. That's why I *must* slap Zverkov's face! I'm obliged to do that. So, that's settled. Now I'm tearing off to give him a slap.'

'Faster!'

The driver jerked the reins.

'I'll do it the moment I go in. But shouldn't I perhaps say a few words before the slap, by way of introduction? No! I'll just walk in and give him one. They'll all be sitting in the lounge and he'll be on the sofa with Olympia. Damn that Olympia! Once she laughed at my face and refused me. I'll drag Olympia to one side by the hair and pull Zverkov along by the ears. No, better by one ear, I'll haul him right round the room by one ear. Very likely they'll all start beating me and throw me out. In fact, that's almost a certainty. Let them – I'll have delivered the first slap: that's my prerogative and according to the code of honour that's everything. He'll be branded for life and no amount of blows will ever wipe out that slap – only a duel. He'll *have* to fight. Well, let them thrash me now. Let them, the base swine! Trudolyubov will lay into me particularly hard – he's so strong. Ferfichkin will pounce on me from the side and almost certainly grab me by the hair. So, let them, let them! That's my whole reason for going. They'll finally have to get into their mutton-heads that there's a whole tragedy here. When they drag me to the door I'll call out loud that they aren't worth my little finger.'

'Faster, driver, faster!' I shouted at the cabby.

He gave a sudden start and flourished his whip. (My shout was a really wild one.)

'We'll fight at dawn, that's settled. I'm finished with the department. A moment ago Ferfichkin said *l*epartment instead of department. But where shall I get pistols? Nonsense! I'll take an advance on my salary and buy them. What about powder and bullets? That's the second's affair. And how can I arrange all this before dawn? And where am I to find a second? I don't have any friends . . .'

'Nonsense!' I shouted, growing increasingly ruffled. 'Nonsense!'

'The first person I ask in the street is obliged to be my second – it's just the same as pulling a drowning man out of the water. The most exceptional circumstances must be allowed for. And even if I were to ask the head of my department himself tomorrow, to be my second, he too would have to agree, simply out of chivalry – and to keep the secret! Anton Antonych . . .'

The fact was, at that very moment I could see more clearly and vividly than anyone in the whole wide world the vile absurdity of my assumptions and the reverse side of the coin, but . . .

'Faster, driver, faster, you rogue!'

'But sir!' groaned that son of the soil.

Suddenly I went cold all over. 'Wouldn't it be better . . . wouldn't it be better to go straight home? God – why did I have to invite myself to that dinner yesterday? No, it's impossible! And all that promenading for three hours, from table to stove? No, they alone, no one else, should pay for all those promenades! They must wipe out the dishonour!'

'Faster!'

'But what if they should hand me over to the police? They wouldn't dare! They'd be afraid of the scandal. And what if Zverkov turns down the duel, out of contempt? That's even highly likely. But then I'll show them . . . I'll dash to the posting-station when he's leaving, grab his leg and rip off his overcoat as he's getting into the coach. Then I'll sink my teeth into his arm. I'll bite him. "Just look, everyone, see to what lengths a desperate man can be driven!" Let him punch me on the head and the others from behind. I'll shout to all the people there: "Just look at this young puppy who's off to captivate Circassian girls with my spit on his face!"

'Of course, after that everything is finished! The department vanishes from the face of the earth. I'm arrested, tried, given the sack and sent to a Siberian penal settlement. But never mind! When I'm released fifteen years later, a beggar, all in rags, I'll drag myself after him. I'll seek him out in some provincial town. He'll be married and happy. He'll have a grown-up daughter . . . I'll tell him: "Look, you monster, just look at my hollow cheeks, look at my rags! I've lost everything – my career, my happiness, art, science, *the woman I loved* – and all because of you. Here are the pistols. I've come to discharge mine – and . . . and . . . I forgive you." Then I'll fire into the air and that's the last he'll hear of me . . .'

I was even on the verge of tears, although at that very moment I knew perfectly well that all this came out of *Silvio*[35] and Lermontov's *Masquerade*.[36] And suddenly I felt terribly ashamed, so ashamed that I stopped the horse, got out of the sledge and stood in the snow in the middle of the street. The cabby looked at me in amazement and took a deep breath.

What could I do? I couldn't possibly go *there* – the whole thing had turned into a farce. And I couldn't leave things as they were, since then there would be . . . Good God! How could I possibly leave things as they were! And after such insults!

'No!' I called out, flinging myself back into the sledge. 'It's predestined, it's fate! Drive on – *there*! Let's go!'

And in my impatience I thumped the driver on the neck with my fist.

'What's that for? What yer 'itting me for?' cried my poor old peasant, but he whipped on his miserable nag, which made it kick out with its hind legs.

The wet snow was falling in large flakes; I unbuttoned my coat – I wasn't concerned about the snow. I had forgotten everything else since I finally decided on the slap and I realized with horror that it was all *bound to happen* right now and that *no power on earth could prevent it*. The solitary street lamps were glimmering mournfully through the snowy haze like torches at a funeral. The snow was packed under my overcoat, under my frock-coat, under my tie and melting there. I didn't bother to cover myself again – after all, it was a lost cause! Finally we arrived. I leapt out, scarcely aware of what I was doing, raced up the steps and started hammering on the door with fists and feet. My legs were becoming terribly weak, especially at the knees. The door seemed to open quickly, as if they knew I was coming. (In actual fact, Simonov had forewarned them that another person might be coming, as it was a place where you had to give prior notice and generally take precautions. It was one of those 'fashion shops' of the time, long since closed down by the police. During the day it was in fact a shop, but in the evenings those with suitable recommendations could go there as guests.) With hurried steps I walked across the dark shop and went into the familiar salon where a single candle was burning and I stopped in bewilderment: no one was there.

'Where are they?' I asked someone.

But of course they'd already managed to disperse . . .

Standing before me was a person with a stupid smile, the madam herself, who knew me slightly. A moment later the door opened and another character appeared.

Without paying attention to anything I paced up and down the room, seemingly talking to myself. It was as if I had been saved from death and I was rejoicing in the fact with my whole being. Indeed, I would most certainly have delivered that slap – most certainly would I have delivered it! But now they weren't there and . . . everything had vanished, everything had changed . . . ! I looked around. Still I couldn't make head or tail of it. Mechanically I glanced at the girl who had come in: before me I saw a fresh, young, rather pale face with straight, dark eyebrows and a serious, as it were faintly surprised expression. This I liked immediately; I would have hated her had she been smiling. I began to stare at her more intently and with some effort, so to speak. I still hadn't collected my thoughts. There was something kind and simple-hearted in that face, but also something somehow strangely serious. I am certain that this was to her disadvantage in that place and that not one of those idiots had noticed her. Besides, she could not have been called a beauty, although she was tall, strong and well-built. She was dressed extremely simply. Suddenly something nasty cut me to the quick. I went straight over to her . . .

By chance I caught sight of myself in the mirror. My agitated face struck me as utterly repulsive: pale, vicious, mean, my hair dishevelled. 'That's fine, I'm glad of it,' I reflected. 'Yes, I'm really glad that I'll strike her as repulsive; that pleases me . . .'

VI

. . . Somewhere behind the partition, as if under immense pressure and as if someone were strangling it, the clock suddenly wheezed. After an unnaturally prolonged wheeze there followed a rather thin, nasty, somewhat unexpectedly rapid chime, as if someone had suddenly leapt forward. It struck two. I regained consciousness, although I hadn't been asleep, merely lying in a half-trance.

In the cramped, narrow, low-ceilinged room, crammed with a huge wardrobe, cluttered with cardboard boxes, rags and all kinds of scraps of clothing, it was almost completely dark. The candle-end on the table at the other end of the room had almost gone out, feebly flickering now and then. In a few minutes the whole room would be completely dark . . .

It did not take me long fully to come to my senses; all at once, without any effort, everything came back to me in a flash, as if it had been lying in wait in order to attack me again. And in that half-conscious state itself there constantly remained a kind of focal point in my memory that hadn't been forgotten at all and around which my sleepy reveries wearily revolved. But the strange thing was that all the events of that day seemed to me now I was awake to have taken place long, long ago, as if I had lived through everything in the remote past.

My head was feeling muzzy. Something seemed to be hovering over me, nagging at me, rousing and disturbing me, Once again, anguish and spleen seethed within me and sought an outlet. All at once I saw right next to me two wide-open eyes surveying me curiously and intently. Their look was cold, indifferent and sullen, like a stranger's. This I found oppressive.

A gloomy thought stirred in my brain and swept through my whole body like some foul sensation, similar to the kind you experience on going into a damp and mouldy cellar. It was somehow unnatural that only at that precise moment did those two eyes decide to start scrutinizing me. I also remembered that in the course of two hours I hadn't spoken one word to that creature and even considered it quite unnecessary; until a few moments before I was even pleased about it for some reason. But now there suddenly and vividly appeared to me, as absurd and repulsive as a spider, a vision of lust which, without love, crudely and shamelessly, begins exactly where true love is crowned. We looked at each other for a long time, but she didn't lower her eyes before mine, nor did she alter her expression, so that finally I was overcome by a kind of eerie feeling.

'What's your name?' I asked brusquely, to get it over with as soon as possible.

'Liza,' she replied, almost in a whisper but somehow quite ungraciously – and she looked away.

For a while I said nothing.

'The weather today . . . snow . . . it's foul!' I muttered almost to myself, wearily putting my hand behind my head and gazing up at the ceiling. She didn't reply. It was all very ugly.

'Are you from St Petersburg?' I asked a moment later, almost in a temper and turning my head slightly towards her.

'No.'

'Where are you from?'

'From Riga,' she replied reluctantly.

'Are you German?'

'Russian.'

'Been here long?'

'Where?'

'In this house?'

'Two weeks.'

She was speaking more and more abruptly. The candle had gone out altogether and I could no longer distinguish her face.

'Are your mother and father alive?'

'Yes . . . no . . . yes, they are.'

'Where are they?'

'There . . . in Riga.'

'Who are they?'

'Just . . .'

'What do you mean "just"? Who are they, what do they do?'

'They're tradespeople.'

'Have you always lived with them?'

'Yes.'

'How old are you?'

'Twenty.'

'Why did you leave them?'

'I just . . .'

This *just* meant: leave me alone, I'm sick of all this. We said nothing.

God knows why I didn't leave. I myself was feeling increasingly depressed and disgusted. Visions of all that had happened the previous day started drifting through my mind, disjointedly, as if of their own accord, against my will. Suddenly I remembered a scene I had witnessed that morning in the street when I was anxiously trotting along to the office.

'This morning they were carrying a coffin out and very nearly dropped it,' I suddenly said out loud, without the slightest wish to start a conversation – almost unintentionally as it were.

'A coffin?'

'Yes, in the Haymarket.[37] They were taking it out of a cellar.'

'Out of a cellar?'

'Well, not exactly a cellar – a basement . . . you know . . . down below . . . from a house of ill fame. There was such filth everywhere . . . eggshells, litter . . . nasty smells . . . it was disgusting.'

Silence.

'A dreadful day for a funeral!' I began again, simply for the sake of saying something.

'Why dreadful?'

'The snow . . . the damp . . .' (I yawned).

'Doesn't make any difference . . .' she said suddenly, after a brief pause.

'No, it's horrible . . .' (I yawned again). 'I'm sure the grave diggers must have been swearing because they were wet from the snow. Most probably there was water in the grave.'

'Why should there be water in the grave?' she asked with some curiosity, but speaking even more rudely and disjointedly than before. Suddenly something spurred me on.

'Well, yes, there's water at the bottom – six inches of it. In Volkovo Cemetery,[38] you can't dig a dry grave.'

'Why is that?'

'What do you mean "why"? Because the whole place is waterlogged. There's marsh everywhere. They just lower them into the water. I've seen it myself . . . many times . . .'

(I had never seen it, nor had I ever been to Volkovo – I'd only heard others talk about it.)

'So it's all the same to you – dying?'

'Why should I die?' she replied, somewhat defensively.

'Well, one day you'll die and I reckon you'll die just like that woman did. She too was a young girl like you . . . died of consumption.'

'A whore would have died in hospital.' (She knows about it already, I reflected – she said 'whore' instead of 'young girl'.)

'She was in debt to the madam,' I continued, warming more and more to the argument, 'and she served her almost right to the end, despite having consumption. The cab drivers around here were telling some soldiers about it. Most likely they were former acquaintances of hers. They were laughing and planning on having a few drinks to her memory in the pub. (Much of this too was my own invention.)

Silence, profound silence. She didn't even stir.

'So, you think it's better to die in hospital?'

'Isn't it all the same . . . And why should I die?' she added irritably.

'If not now, then later on.'

'All right, later on . . .'

'But things don't work out like that! You're young now, pretty and fresh – that's why you're worth quite a lot to them. But another year of this kind of life and you won't be the same, you'll fade away.'

'After a year?'

'At any rate, after a year you'll be worth less,' I continued sadistically. 'You'll have to leave here for somewhere even lower, another house. A year after that – to a third house, sinking lower and lower and about seven years later you'll end up in a cellar in the Haymarket. That wouldn't be so bad, but the trouble is if on top of that you contracted some illness, let's say, a weak chest . . . or caught a cold, or something. In that sort of life it's very hard to shake off an illness. It will take a grip on you and you won't be able to get rid of it. And then you'll die.'

'So, I'll die,' she replied, very bad-temperedly and with a quick change of position.

'But I feel sorry.'

'Sorry for whom?'

'Sorry for the life you're leading.'

Silence.

'Did you ever have a boyfriend? Eh?'

'What's it to do with you?'

'Well, I'm not interrogating you, I'd just like to know. Why are you so angry? Of course, you probably had your share of trouble. Why should I care? I just feel sorry.'

'For whom?'

'Sorry for you.'

'There's no point . . .' she whispered almost inaudibly and she restlessly shifted about again.

This immediately made me see red. So! I had been so gentle with her, but she . . .

'Well, what do you think? That you're on the right path, eh?'

'I don't think anything.'

'Well, that's bad, not thinking anything. Open your eyes while there's still time. And there *is* time. You're still young, pretty, you could fall in love, get married and be happy . . .'

'Not all married women are happy . . .' she cut me short with her rude patter of before.

'Of course not all, but it's still a good sight better than being here. Incomparably better. And where there's love you can even live without happiness. Life is sweet, even in sorrow. It's good to be alive in this world, however you live. But what's here except . . . a foul stench? Ugh!'

I turned away, disgusted. I was no longer coolly rational: I myself was beginning to be affected by what I was saying and I was becoming heated. I was longing to expound those cherished *little ideas* that I had nurtured in my corner. Suddenly something caught fire within me, some kind of purpose 'revealed' itself.

'Don't take any notice of my being here, I'm no example for you. Perhaps I'm even worse than you. However, I was drunk when I came here,' I added, hurrying to excuse myself all the same. 'Besides, a man is no example for a woman at all. They're totally different. Although I may degrade and dirty myself, I'm no one's slave. I came here – and then I'll be gone. I can shake it all off and again be a different man. But consider the fact that you're a slave right from the start. Yes, a slave! You give everything up, your entire freedom. And later, if you want to break these chains, it will be too late: the fetters will bind you tighter and tighter. And it's such a damnable chain! I know it. And I'm not talking about anything else, as you probably wouldn't even understand. Now tell me this: you must already be in debt to your mistress, eh? There, you see!' I added, although she didn't answer but simply listened in silence with her whole being . . . There's a chain, for you! You'll never pay her off. That's what happens. Same as selling your soul to the devil . . .

'And besides, for all you know, I might be a miserable wretch like you and I'm deliberately wallowing in muck because I'm sick at heart too. Sorrow drives people to drink, so I'm here – out of sorrow. Now tell me – what's good about all this? You and I . . . we made love just a few moments ago . . . and the whole time we didn't say one word to each other and afterwards you began staring at me like a wild woman. And I stared back. Is that the way to love? It's really shocking, that's what!'

'Yes,' she agreed, sharply and hastily. The hastiness of that 'yes' even surprised me. Was the same thought perhaps running through her mind just then, when she was watching me? Did it mean that she too was capable of some thought . . . ?

'Damn it, this is very curious, this *kinship*,' I thought, almost rubbing my hands. And how could she fail to cope, with such a young spirit as hers . . . ?'

It was the game more than anything that appealed to me.

She had turned her head closer to me and in the darkness seemed to be leaning on her elbow. Perhaps she was scrutinizing me? How sorry I was that I couldn't distinguish her eyes . . . I could hear her heavy breathing.

'Why did you come here?' I began, now with a certain authority.

'Because . . .'

'I suppose it was nice, living in a family home, so warm and free – your own little nest!'

'And supposing it was worse than here?'

The thought: 'I must strike the right note' flashed through my mind, 'sentimentality probably won't get me very far with her.'

However, it was just a passing thought. I swear that she really did interest me. Besides, I was feeling rather relaxed and in the mood. After all, knavery gets on so easily with sentiment.

'Who can tell?' I hastened to reply. 'Anything is possible. You see, I'm convinced that someone wronged you and *they* were more to blame than you were. You see, I know nothing of your background, but a girl like you doesn't end up in a place like this because she wants to, does she?'

'So, what kind of girl am I?' she whispered barely audibly – but I could make out what she said.

"To hell with it, I'm flattering her! That's low of me. Or perhaps it's all right . . ." She remained silent.

'Look here, Liza, I'll tell you about myself. If I'd grown up in a family when I was a child, I wouldn't be as I am now. I often think about it. You see, however bad it may be in a family, they're still your own father and mother and not your enemies, not strangers, even though they may show their love for you just once a year. At any rate, you can be sure that you're at home. I grew up without any family – that's certainly why I turned out the way I am – without feelings.'

Again I waited for her to speak.

'Perhaps she doesn't understand,' I thought. 'What's more, she must find all this moralizing rather comical.'

'If I were a father and had a daughter I think I'd love the daughter more than a son really, I would,' I began obliquely, as if on another subject, to divert her attention. I was blushing, I do confess.

'Why's that?' she asked.

Ah! So she was listening!

'Well, I don't really know, Liza. You see, once I knew a father who was a very strict, grim kind of man, but he used to kneel before his daughter and kiss her hands and feet. Really, he couldn't stop feasting his eyes on her. She'd be dancing at a party and he'd stand in the same spot for hours without taking his eyes off her. He was besotted with her – that I can understand. At night, when she was tired and fell asleep, he'd wake up and go and kiss her in her sleep and make the sign of the cross over her. He went around in a greasy old frock-coat, was tight-fisted towards everyone else, but he would spend his last copeck on her, buy her expensive presents – and the joy it brought him if the gift was to her liking! Fathers always love their daughters more than a mother does. For some girls home is a very happy place. But I don't think I would let a daughter of mine get married.'

'But why not?' she asked with the faintest of laughs.

'I'd be jealous, really! How could she kiss someone else, love a stranger more than her father? The thought of it pains me. Of course, all this is nonsense, in the end everyone comes to see reason. But I think that before letting her marry I'd have exhausted myself with worry; I'd have found fault with every suitor. However, in the end I'd let her marry the one she loved. You see, the man the daughter falls in love with always strikes the father as worst of all. It's always been like that. It causes a lot of trouble in families.'

'Others are glad to sell their daughters rather than give them in marriage honestly,' she suddenly said.

Ah! So that was it!

'That only happens in those cursed families where there's neither God nor love, Liza,' I threw in heatedly. 'For where there's no love there's no reason. There are such families, that's true, but it's not them I'm talking about. From what you say you can't have known any kindness in your family. You are a genuinely unfortunate person. Hm . . . all that mainly comes about through poverty.'

'And is it any better among gentlefolk? Honest folk can live decently even if they're poor.'

'Hm . . . yes, perhaps so. But there's something else, Liza: people only like to count their sorrows and not their good fortune. But if they were to take account of things as they should then they'd see that everyone has his fair share laid in store for him. So, supposing all goes well with your family, if God gives his blessing, if your husband turns out to be a good man, who loves you, cherishes you and doesn't leave you! Life is so good in that family! And sometimes it's good even if one half of it is beset with sorrow. And is there anywhere without sorrow? Should you marry perhaps you'll *find out for yourself*. But then consider the early days of married life to the man you love: what happiness sometimes comes along! And that happens time and again. In the early days even quarrels with the husband end happily. Sometimes, the more a woman loves her husband the more quarrels she picks with him. It's true; I once knew someone like that. "You know I love you very much", she would say, "and it's because I love you that I torment you, so that you can feel it." Do you know that someone can deliberately torment another, out of love? Mainly women do that. The woman thinks to herself: but then I'll be so tender and loving to him afterwards that it's no sin if I make him suffer a little now! And everyone in the house is happy for you, everything is so good, so happy, so peaceful and honest . . . And there's others who are jealous as well – I knew one like that – if the husband went out somewhere she couldn't bear it and in the middle of the night she'd leap out of bed and go snooping about to discover whether he was there, in that house, with that woman. That's very bad. And she knows it's bad and her heart sinks and she blames herself; but she loves him – it's all for love. And how good it is to make peace after a quarrel, to admit that it was her fault and to forgive him! And how good it is for both of them, how good everything suddenly becomes – just as if they were newly met, newly wed and their love was born anew. And nobody, positively nobody, need know what goes on between husband and wife if they love each other. Whatever quarrels they get into they should never summon their own mother as judge, when they each tell tales about the other. They are their own judges. Love is a divine mystery and must be kept hidden from all other eyes, no matter what happens. That way it's holier, it's better. They respect each other more and much is founded on respect. And if once there was love, if they married for love, why should love ever pass? Is it really impossible to keep it alive? Those cases are rare when it's impossible to keep it alive. And if the husband succeeds in being a good and honest man, how could love ever fade? It's true, the first, conjugal love passes, but then even finer love comes along. Their souls will be as one and they will do all things together; they will hold no secrets from one another. And when children come along, every moment, even the hardest, will seem like happiness. As long as they love one another and are steadfast. And then work itself is a joy – even if you sometimes have to go hungry for your children that's a joy too. For they will love you for it later, as it means you're storing things up for yourself. As the children grow up you feel that you're setting them an example, that you're a support to them; that were you to die they will carry your thoughts and feelings with them, all their lives, since they have received from you your image and taken your likeness. That means it's an immense duty. So, in this case, how can the father and mother not grow closer together? Do they say that having children is a great burden? Who says this? It's heavenly bliss! Do you love little children, Liza? I love them, terribly. Just think – a tiny, rosy baby sucking at your breast – well, every husband's heart must turn to his wife when he sees her sitting there with his little child. A rosy, chubby little baby, stretching itself and snuggling up to you. Those plump little arms, those tiny clean nails – so tiny it makes you laugh to look at them; little eyes that seem already to understand everything. And it sucks away, the tiny hand plucking playfully at your breast. Father comes over and it tears itself from the breast, leans over backwards, looks up at the father and laughs – it's so screamingly funny – again, again, it goes on sucking. And then it might suddenly go and bite the mother's breast, if it's already teething, and artfully look at her with its little eyes as if to say: "Look, I've bitten you!" Surely that's the height of happiness when all three – husband, wife and baby – are together? Much can be forgiven for those moments. No, Liza, you must first learn to live yourself, and then you can blame others!'

'It's with little pictures, it's with these little pictures that you must show her!' I thought to myself, although I really was speaking with genuine feeling. And suddenly I blushed. 'What if she suddenly bursts out laughing; where shall I put myself then?' The very thought drove me into a frenzy. Towards the end of my speech I'd become positively heated and now my vanity was suffering somewhat. The silence dragged on. I felt like giving her a little shove.

'What are you on about?' she said and then stopped.

But now I understood everything: in her voice there sounded a different note, tremulous, not harsh or rude and defiant as before, but somehow soft and bashful – indeed, so bashful that I myself felt ashamed and guilty.

'What did you say?' I asked with tender curiosity.

'Well, you . . .'

'What?'

'Well, you . . . sound just like a book,' she said and again I seemed to detect a hint of mockery in her voice.

This remark cut me to the quick. I hadn't been expecting that. And I didn't understand that she was deliberately using that mockery as a mask and that this was the last subterfuge of those who have been subjected to vulgar and persistent probing, of those who out of pride will not yield until the very last moment and who are afraid of unbosoming themselves in front of you. From the very timidity with which she made several attempts at mockery and only then finally brought herself to speak out I should have been able to guess this. But I didn't guess and I was gripped by feelings of spite.

'Just you wait,' I thought.

VII

'That's enough, Liza. What do books have to do with it when I'm feeling rotten on your behalf? Or perhaps it isn't on your behalf?

'I've only just woken up to all this myself . . . Surely, surely, you yourself must find it loathsome here? But apparently not – habit counts for a lot! The devil only knows what habit can do to a person. You don't seriously think, do you, that you'll never grow old, that you'll always stay pretty and that they'll keep you on for ever and ever? And I'm not talking about the dirty tricks they play, here . . . However, I'm going to tell you this, about your present life here. You're still young, comely, attractive, with spirit and feelings. Well, do you know, as I came to just now I immediately felt disgusted at being here with you? You need to be drunk to come to this sort of place. If you happened to be somewhere else, living as normal, decent people live, I'd not only run after you – I'd positively fall in love with you and be glad of one look from you, let alone one word. I'd be waiting for you by your gate, I'd go down on my knees to you; I'd look on you as my bride-to-be and consider myself honoured. I wouldn't dare harbour one unclean thought about you. But here I know very well that I only have to whistle and whether you like it or not you'll come to me, as it wouldn't be *me* who has to do your bidding, but you would have to do mine. Even the meanest peasant can hire himself out, but he won't be enslaving himself altogether, because he knows it's just for a limited time. But where's your limited time? Just think what it is you're giving up here, what you are enslaving! It's your soul, your soul, over which you have no command that you are enslaving, together with your body! You let your love be desecrated by any old drunkard. Love! – that's everything, that's a precious jewel, a virgin's treasure – love! Some men are ready to sacrifice their souls or go to their deaths to earn that love. And what is your love worth now? You are sold, every part of you, and why should anyone try to win your love when he can get all he wants without any love? There's no worse insult for a young girl than that, do you understand? I've heard people say that to keep you silly fools happy they let you have lovers here. But that's just to spoil you, it's downright deceit, they're only laughing at you – and you believe them. And does this lover in fact love you? I think not. How can he love you when he knows you might be called away from him at any moment? He'd be a filthy devil to do that! But how can he have one drop of respect for you? What do you have in common with him? He'll laugh at you and steal from you – that's what his love amounts to! And you'll be lucky if he doesn't beat you. Or maybe he will. And if you have one of those gentlemen with you, just go and ask if he'll marry you. Yes, he'll laugh right in your face – that is, if he doesn't spit at you or knock you down. And perhaps he's not worth more than a brass farthing himself. And for *what* have you ruined your life here? To be plied with coffee and given plenty to eat? And why do they feed you so well? Any decent woman wouldn't allow one crumb to pass her lips for she'd know very well *why* they're feeding her. In this place you're in debt and you'll always be in debt, right up to the very end, up to the time when customers give you a wide berth. And that time isn't far off – don't rely on your youth. You see, in this kind of place all that passes in a flash. They'll throw you out. And not simply throw you out, since long before that they'll have started finding fault with you, reproaching you, cursing you, as though it wasn't *you* who sacrificed your health and allowed your youth and soul to perish for madam's benefit, but as if you'd ruined *her*, robbed her, sent her out begging. And don't expect any support: the others, your friends, will also turn against you, so that they can get into her good books, because everyone here is a slave and has lost all conscience and sense of compassion long ago. They are defiled and there's nothing on earth more repulsive, obscene and offensive than their abuse. And you'll have given up everything, everything – your health, youth, beauty, your hopes, with no redemption and at twenty-two you'll look like thirty-five and you'll be lucky if you still have your health – pray to God for that! Perhaps you're thinking now that it's not really work you're doing, that it's all one long holiday! But in fact there is no work in the world harder or more back-breaking and there never has been. Anyone would think it's enough to make you cry your heart out. And you won't dare utter a word, not one syllable when they turn you out and you'll leave as if it were all your fault. And you'll move on to another place, then to a third, then somewhere else, until finally you end up in the Haymarket. And there they'll beat you as a matter of course; that's their way of welcoming you. The customers just can't fondle a woman without first giving her a good thrashing. You don't believe that it's so awful there? Well, just you go along some time and take a look for yourself – then you might see with your own eyes. One New Year's Day I saw one of those women standing by a door. She'd been turned out in ridicule by her own people to cool off a bit because of her dreadful howling and they'd locked the door behind her. By nine o'clock in the morning she was already dead drunk, dishevelled, half-naked and bruised all over. Her face was powdered, but she was black all around the eyes. She was bleeding from nose and mouth – some cabby had given her a bashing. She sat down on the stone doorsteps holding some kind of salted fish and howling, as if bemoaning her "lot", banging the fish against the steps. A crowd of cabbies and drunken soldiers stood in the doorway taunting her. You don't believe that you'll end up like her? And I wouldn't like to believe it either, but how do you know? Perhaps eight or ten years before, that same woman with the salted fish arrived here fresh from somewhere, pure and innocent as a cherub, knowing no evil and blushing at every word . . . Perhaps she was just like you – proud, sensitive, unlike the others, looking like a queen, aware that perfect bliss was awaiting the man who fell in love with her and whom she fell in love with. But you see how it all ended? And what if at that very moment when, drunk and dishevelled, she was banging that fish against the filthy steps – what if at that very moment she recalled all those pure, earlier years spent at her father's house, when she went to school and a neighbour's son waited for her on the road and assured her that he would love her all his life and place his destiny in her hands? And when they pledged their love for each other for ever and would marry as soon as they grew up? No, Liza, it would be a blessing, a real blessing if you died of consumption in some corner or cellar, like that girl I was telling you about. In hospital, you say? All right, if they take you there, but what if your mistress still needs you? Consumption is an odd sort of illness: it's not like a fever. A person suffering from that might go on hoping to the very last minute and say she's well. She reassures herself – and that suits your mistress. Don't worry, it's true. It means you've sold your soul and you owe money into the bargain, so you daren't utter a word. And when you're dying they'll all desert you, turn their backs on you, because what use are you to them? What's more, they'll take you to task for using up space for nothing and not getting on with your job and dying. You'll have to beg for a drink and they'll curse when they give it you. "When are you going to kick the bucket, you slut! You keep us awake, you never stop moaning and the customers won't go anywhere near you." It's true; I myself have overheard things like that. And when you're actually dying they'll shove you in the most foul-smelling corner of the cellar, in the dark and damp. And what will you be thinking, as you lie there all alone? You'll die and you'll be carted off in a hurry, by impatient, grumbling strangers. No one will say a prayer for you, no one will sigh for you – all they'll want is to get you off their backs as quickly as they can. They'll buy a cheap coffin and then they'll go and carry you out like that poor girl today and then they'll go and say prayers for you in the pub. There'll be slush, rubbish and slime in the grave – the gravediggers won't stand on ceremony for the likes of you. "Let 'er down, Vanyukha. Well, just 'er luck, even now she's got 'er legs up in the air, that's the sort she was. Now, shorten the ropes and stop mucking about." "She's all right as she is ain't she?" "All right, you say? Can't you see she's lying on 'er side? She were a 'uman being once, weren't she? Oh, go on then, fill it in." And they won't waste much time arguing because of you. They'll hurry up and shovel the wet blue clay over you and then it's off to the pub. And that'll be the last anyone will remember about you in this world. Children, fathers and husbands go to other women's graves, but for you there'll be no tears, no sighs, no memorial prayers and no one, no one in the whole world will ever come to visit you. Your name will vanish from the face of the earth, as if you'd never even existed, never been born! There'll only be mud and swamp and you can knock as much as you like on your coffin lid at night when the dead awaken: "Let me out, kind folk, so I can live in the world again! Once I lived but I didn't see life, I frittered it away, I drank it away in a pub in the Haymarket. Set me free, kind folk, I want to live in the world again . . . !"'

I had laid it on so thick I felt a lump rising in my throat . . . and suddenly I stopped, raised myself a little in fright, bowed my head apprehensively and my heart pounded as I started listening: I had good reason to feel confused.

For some time I'd had the feeling that I'd brought about a great spiritual upheaval in her and broken her heart, and the more certain I was of this the more eager I was to achieve my goal as quickly and comprehensively as possible. It was the game, the game that fascinated me. However, it wasn't only the game . . .

I knew I was speaking in a stiff, artificial, even bookish manner – in brief, I couldn't talk in any other way except 'just like a book'. But it wasn't that which troubled me: after all, I knew, I felt that I would be understood and that this very bookishness might perhaps advance my cause. But now it had made such an impact my nerve suddenly failed me. No, never, never before had I witnessed such despair! She lay there prone, her face buried in the pillow, clasping it with both hands. Her bosom was heaving. Her whole young body was violently shaking, as if she were having convulsions. Stifled sobs constricted her chest, then they rent it – and suddenly they broke free in wails and shrieks. And then she pressed her face even more firmly against the pillow: she didn't want anyone there, not a single living soul, to know of her sufferings and tears. She bit the pillow, bit her hand until it bled (I noticed this later), clutching at her tangled plaits and weakening from the effort, holding her breath and clenching her teeth. I was about to speak to her, to beg her to calm herself, but I felt that I simply didn't dare and suddenly, in a fit of violent trembling, almost in terror, I began groping around for my clothes so that I could somehow get dressed and leave as soon as possible. It was dark, and hard as I tried I couldn't get my clothes on quickly. Suddenly I found a box of matches and a candlestick with a new candle.

The moment the light filled the room Liza suddenly leapt up and sat looking at me almost vacantly, with a half-demented smile on her distorted face. I sat down beside her and took her hands. She came to her senses, threw herself towards me as if wanting to clasp me in her arms, but she did not dare and quietly bowed her head before me.

'Liza, my dear, I didn't mean to . . . please forgive me,' I began, but she squeezed my hand in hers so violently that I guessed I was saying the wrong thing and I stopped.

'Here's my address, Liza, come and see me.'

'I will!' she whispered emphatically, but without raising her head.

'And now I'm going . . . goodbye . . . until we meet again.'

I stood up and so did she, and then suddenly, blushing furiously, she shuddered, seized the shawl that was lying on the chair and flung it over her shoulders, covering herself up to the chin. Then she smiled again rather painfully, blushed and gave me a strange look. I felt dreadful; I was in a hurry to leave, to get right away from that place.

'Wait a moment,' she said suddenly when we were already at the entrance hall door; holding me back with one hand on my overcoat she hastily put down the candle and ran off – clearly she had remembered something or wanted to bring something to show me. As she did so her face was flushed, her eyes were sparkling and there was a smile on her lips – what could it be? Reluctantly I waited. After a minute she returned with a look that seemed to be begging forgiveness for something. Altogether this was no longer the same face or the same look as before – so sullen, distrustful, obstinate. Now her look was imploring, gentle and at the same time trusting, warm and timid. That was the way children look at those whom they love very much and from whom they are asking for something. Her eyes were hazel, so beautiful, alive, capable of expressing both love and sullen hatred.

Without offering me a word of explanation, as if I were some higher being who understood everything without the need for explanation, she handed me a piece of paper. At that moment her whole face was radiant with the most naive, almost childlike exultation. I unfolded the letter. It was from a medical student, or someone like that, a terribly high-flown and flowery, but extremely polite declaration of love. I can't recall the precise wording, but I do remember very well that through the elevated style one could distinguish the kind of genuine feeling that cannot be feigned. When I had read it through I met her ardent, inquisitive and childishly impatient gaze. Her eyes were glued to my face as she impatiently waited to hear what I had to say. In a few hurried words, but somehow joyfully, almost proud of the fact, she explained that she had gone to a party at the house of 'some very, very nice people – *family people* – where they *still knew* nothing, absolutely nothing', as she was still fairly new there and only . . . but that she was far from deciding whether to stay but would definitely leave once she had repaid her debt . . . "So, this student had been there and danced with her the whole evening. He talked to her and it turned out that he had known her when they were children in Riga, that they'd played together, but that was a long time ago. And he'd known her parents, but knew absolutely nothing *about this* and suspected nothing. And the very next day after the party (three days ago) he had sent her that letter through the friend who had gone to the party with her . . . and . . . well . . . that was all."

When she had finished her story she dropped her sparkling eyes rather bashfully.

Poor girl, she was keeping that student's letter as a treasure and had run off to fetch this, her only treasure, reluctant that I should leave without knowing that she was loved, honourably and sincerely, that even *she* was spoken to respectfully. That letter was certainly destined to lie in a box, without any consequences. But that didn't matter. I am certain she would treasure it all her life, as her pride and justification and now, at this moment, she had remembered that letter and fetched it in all naivety to show off in front of me, to resurrect herself in my eyes, so that I would praise her after seeing it. I said nothing, pressed her hand and left. I was dying to get away . . . I walked the whole way home, although the snow was still falling in large, wet flakes. I was exhausted, crushed, perplexed. But the truth was already shining through the perplexity. The vile truth!

VIII

However, it took some time before I was prepared to acknowledge that truth. Waking next morning after a few hours of deep, leaden sleep and immediately mulling over all the events of the previous day, I was even astonished at my *sentimentality* with Liza and then at all those 'horrors and miseries of yesterday'. 'Phew, a fine attack of womanish nerves!' I thought. 'And what possessed me to foist my address on her? What if she came? Well, let her come, it doesn't matter . . .' But *evidently* that wasn't the most important, the most urgent matter now: what I needed to do was to hurry up and – at any price and as soon as possible – to salvage my reputation in the eyes of Zverkov and Simonov. That was the most important thing. And in my frantic activity that morning I forgot all about Liza.

First of all I had to repay yesterday's debt to Simonov without further delay. I decided on a desperate measure: to borrow the entire fifteen roubles from Anton Antonych. Luckily, he was in the best of moods that morning and gave me the money the moment I asked. I was so delighted with this that as I signed the IOU with a somewhat jaunty air I *casually* informed him that the previous day I had been 'living it up with some friends at the Hôtel de Paris where we were seeing off an old friend, one might even say a childhood friend and – you know – a hard drinker, a spoilt darling, but of course of good family, very well off, with a brilliant career, witty, a good chap in fact, always intriguing with certain ladies – you know what I mean; we drank the extra "half dozen" and . . .' Well, no harm done. All this was spoken with the greatest ease, familiarity and smugness.

The moment I arrived home I wrote to Simonov.

To this day I am lost in admiration when I recall the truly gentlemanly, genial and frank tone of my letter. Deftly, nobly and – most importantly – without one superfluous word I had blamed myself for everything. I excused myself – 'if I still may be permitted to excuse myself' – by the fact, that, being completely unused to drink, the very first glass I had (allegedly) drunk before they arrived, while I was waiting for them in the Hôtel de Paris from five to six o'clock, had gone to my head. I apologized chiefly to Simonov and asked him to convey my apologies to all the others, especially to Zverkov, whom I vaguely remembered having insulted. I added that I would have called on all of them personally, but that my head was splitting and, most of all, I was deeply ashamed. I was particularly pleased with a certain 'lightness of touch', even verging on the casual (perfectly polite, however), which suddenly found expression through my pen and which gave them at once to understand better than any possible argument that I took a rather detached view of 'that beastly affair of yesterday'. By no means, not by any reckoning, was I finished outright as you're no doubt thinking, gentlemen, but on the contrary, I look upon the affair as any coolly self-respecting gentlemen ought. Yes, let bygones be bygones!

'Isn't there even a touch of marquis-like playfulness here?' I said admiringly, reading the letter over again. And all because I'm such an intellectually mature and educated person! Other men in my position wouldn't have known how to get themselves out of this mess, but just look how I've managed to extricate myself and now I can start living it up again – and all because I'm a 'mature and educated man of our time'. Yes indeed, very likely it was all because of yesterday's alcohol. Hm . . . well, no . . . not because of alcohol. I didn't touch a drop of vodka between five and six while I was waiting for them. I'd told Simonov a lie – I'd lied shamelessly. And even now I don't feel ashamed . . .

Anyway, to hell with it! The important thing was that I'd got out of it.

I put six roubles in the letter, sealed it and asked Apollon to take it to Simonov. Learning that there was money in the letter, Apollon became more respectful and agreed to go. Towards evening I went out for a stroll. My head was still aching and going round from last night. But the more evening drew on and the thicker the twilight grew, the more my impressions changed and grew muddled – and after them my thoughts. Something deep inside me, in the very depths of my heart and conscience, refused to die and proclaimed itself in burning anguish. For the most part I knocked around the most crowded shopping streets – the Meshchanskaya, the Sadovaya, and near the Yusupov Gardens.[39] I have always been particularly fond of strolling along these streets at dusk, just when crowds of workers and tradespeople returning home from their daily labours are at their thickest, their faces careworn to the point of anger. It was precisely that common bustle, the blatantly prosaic nature of it all, that appealed to me On this occasion all that jostling in the streets only irritated me even more. I could no longer cope, I couldn't find a way out. Something was rising, constantly and painfully rising in my soul, and wouldn't calm down. Positively distraught, I went home. It was as if I had some crime weighing on my conscience.

The thought that Liza might come was a constant torment. I found it strange that of all the memories of yesterday it was hers that particularly tormented me, somehow quite separately. By evening I had managed to forget all the rest, to shrug it off, and I still remained satisfied with my letter to Simonov. But even here I didn't really feel so very satisfied. It was as if I were tormenting myself with Liza alone. 'What if she comes?' I couldn't stop thinking. 'Ah well, let her come. Hm. Only, the rotten thing is, she'll see how I live, for instance. Yesterday I made myself out to be such a . . . hero . . . but now, hm! It's really shocking, though, the way I've let myself go. The flat has such a poverty-stricken look. And how could I possibly have gone out to dinner yesterday in a suit like that! And my oilskin sofa with the stuffing sticking out! And my dressing-gown with which I can't even cover myself up! What rags . . . And she'll see everything – and she'll see Apollon. That swine's bound to insult her. Just to be rude to me he'll start picking on her. And as usual I'll play the coward of course, shuffling around in front of her and wrapping my dressing-gown skirts around me; I'll start smiling and I'll tell lies. Ugh! How vile! And that's not the vilest thing! There's something more important, even viler, even more despicable! Yes, more despicable! Again, once again, I'll don that dishonest, lying mask! . . .'

Having arrived at this thought I simply flared up. 'Why dishonest? What's dishonest about it? I was being quite sincere in what I said yesterday. I remember, my feelings were genuine too. I only wanted to arouse noble sentiments in her . . . if she cried a little that was a good thing, it was bound to have a salutary effect . . .'

All the same, in no way could I rest easy.

The whole of that evening, after I had returned home, even after nine o'clock, when I reckoned that there was no chance of her coming, the thought of her still haunted me and for the main part I remembered her in exactly the same situation. To be precise, one moment from all that had happened yesterday stood out particularly vividly in my memory: that was when I struck a match and saw her pale, distorted face, with that martyred look in her eyes. How pathetic, how unnatural, how twisted her smile had been at that moment! But I couldn't know then that fifteen years later I would still go on picturing Liza to myself with precisely the same twisted, superfluous smile she wore at that moment.

Next day I was again prepared to consider the whole thing nonsense, the result of frayed nerves and above all as an *exaggeration*. I had always acknowledged that as my weak spot and sometimes I feared it greatly. 'I keep exaggerating everything and that's my downfall,' I would repeat to myself hourly. But 'however, Liza will very likely come all the same' – that was the refrain with which all my reasoning invariably concluded at the time. I was so terribly anxious that occasionally I would fly into a mad rage. 'She'll come, she's bound to come!' I would exclaim, dashing round the room, 'if not today then tomorrow and she'll find me!' For that's the typical damned romanticism of all these *pure hearts*! Oh, the loathsomeness, the stupidity, the narrow-mindedness of these 'vile, sentimental souls'! Well, how can she not understand, how is it she doesn't even appear to understand! . . . ?' But at this point I would stop, feeling greatly confused.

'And how few words, how few words were really necessary,' I thought in passing, 'how little need there was of the idyllic (and such an artificial, bookish and contrived idyll at that) in order immediately to shape a human being's entire soul the way I wanted. That's chastity for you! That's virgin soil for you!'

At times I considered going to see her myself, to 'tell her everything' and beg her not to come and see me. But at the very thought of it such anger would seethe within me that I could have crushed that 'damned' Liza if she were suddenly to appear at my side. I would have insulted her, humiliated her, driven her away, struck her!

However, one day passed, then another, a third and still she didn't come and I began to relax. I became particularly cheerful and carefree after nine o'clock; sometimes I even began having dreams – and rather sweet ones at that! for example: 'I'm saving Liza precisely by virtue of the fact that she's coming to see me and I'm talking to her . . . I'm developing her, educating her. Finally I notice that she loves me, loves me passionately. I pretend not to understand (I don't know why I'm pretending, though – probably for a little embellishment). Finally, in complete confusion, beautiful, trembling and sobbing, she throws herself at my feet and tells me that I am her saviour and that she loves me more than anything else in the world. I am amazed, but . . . "Liza," I say, "surely you don't think I haven't noticed that you love me? I saw everything, I guessed, but I didn't dare to be the first to encroach upon your heart, because I influenced you and was afraid that you would deliberately force yourself to respond to my love out of gratitude, that you would try to force emotions that possibly don't exist. But I didn't want that since that is . . . despotism . . . That's indelicate" (well, in short, here I am blathering away with some variety of European, George Sandish, inexpressibly noble finesse . . .). "But now, now – you are mine, you are my creation, pure and beautiful . . . you are my lovely wife.

> And boldly and freely
> Enter my house, mistress of all!" '[40]

And then we start living happily ever after, go abroad, etc, etc. In brief, the whole thing became so vile for me that I would end up by sticking out my tongue at myself.

'And they won't let her out, "the slut",' I thought. 'After all, I don't think they let them go out very much, least of all in the evenings (for some reason I invariably felt that she would come in the evening, at exactly seven o'clock). However, she did say that she wasn't entirely under their thumb and that she had special privileges; that means – hm! What the hell, she'll come, she's bound to come!'

Fortunately at that time Apollon was there to distract me with his boorishness. He tried my patience to the limit. He was the plague of my life, a scourge visited upon me by Providence. For years on end he and I had been constantly at loggerheads and I hated him. God, how I hated him! I don't think I've ever in my life hated anyone as much as him, especially at certain moments. He was a pompous, middle-aged man who did occasional tailoring. For some reason he despised me, even beyond all measure, and treated me with intolerable condescension. However, he looked down on everyone. You only had to take one look at that sleek, flaxen head, at that quiff greased with vegetable oil that stuck up over his forehead, at that solid mouth always pursed into a 'V' shape, and you felt you were in the presence of some creature perpetually bristling with self-assurance. He was a pedant in the highest degree, the greatest pedant I had ever met on this earth; and besides that, his vanity was perhaps worthy only of an Alexander of Macedon. He was enamoured of every single one of his buttons, every single fingernail – oh yes, truly infatuated – that was him in a nutshell! He treated me utterly despotically, spoke to me very seldom and if he did sometimes bring himself to glance at me, it was with a firm, majestically self-assured and invariably supercilious look that sometimes drove me into a frenzy. He performed his duties in a way that suggested he was doing me an enormous favour. However, he hardly ever lifted a finger for me and didn't even consider himself in the least obliged to do anything. Without a shadow of doubt, he looked upon me as the greatest fool on earth and if he 'retained me' it was solely because he could receive his monthly salary from me. He had agreed 'to do nothing' for me, for seven roubles a month. Many sins will be forgiven me for his sake. Sometimes my hatred reached such fever pitch that his walk alone almost sent me into convulsions. But the thing I loathed most of all was the way he lisped. His tongue was a little too long, or something like that, so that he was always lisping and hissing, of which he seemed inordinately proud, imagining that it lent him an extraordinary degree of distinction. He spoke in soft, measured tones, his arms folded behind his back and his eyes fixed on the ground. It particularly infuriated me when he started reading from the psalter behind the partition. I endured many a battle over those recitations. He was passionately fond of reading in the evening in his quiet, drawling voice, as if he were chanting over a corpse. Curiously that's what he ended up doing: now he's employed to read psalms over the dead and he also exterminates rats and makes boot polish. But at that time I couldn't dismiss him, as his existence seemed chemically fused to mine. Besides, on no account would he have agreed to leave. I couldn't live in furnished rooms: my flat was my private property, my shell, my container, in which I hid myself from all humanity, and Apollon, the devil knows why, seemed to be part and parcel of that flat and for seven whole years I couldn't get rid of him.

To keep back his wages, for example, for two or even three days, was out of the question. He would have made such a fuss that I shouldn't have known what to do with myself. But in those days I was feeling so embittered towards everyone that I decided for some reason or other to *punish* Apollon by stopping his wages for a fortnight. I had been intending to do this for a long time, for two years, simply to show him that he should not presume to lord it over me and that I could always stop his wages if I wanted to. I proposed not to mention it to him and even deliberately remained silent in order to conquer his pride and compel him to be first to raise the subject of wages. Then I would take all seven roubles out of a drawer, show him that I had them and was putting them aside because 'I didn't want to, I didn't want to, I simply didn't want to pay him his wages because *that's what I wanted*', because those were 'the Master's wishes', because he was disrespectful, because he was an oaf; but if he were to ask me politely, then I might perhaps relent and pay him; if not, he'd have to wait another fortnight, three weeks – he'd have to wait a whole month . . .

But for all my anger he still got the better of me. I couldn't even hold out for four days. He would begin the way he always did in similar cases, as there *had* been similar cases before; it had all been tried and tested (let me point out that I knew all this in advance, I knew his underhand tactics by heart), that's to say: he would start by keeping his extremely severe glance riveted on me, without dropping it, for several minutes on end, especially when he let me in or out of the flat. If, for instance, I didn't flinch and pretended not to notice these stares, he would, still maintaining his silence, embark on further torments. Suddenly, for no earthly reason, he would glide quietly into my room while I was walking about or reading, stop by the door, put one hand behind his back, part his legs and fix his stare on me – a stare not so much severe as highly contemptuous. If I should suddenly ask what he wanted, he would say nothing, continue staring straight at me for a few more seconds and with those peculiarly pursed lips and a very significant look, slowly turn round and slowly retire to his room. Two hours later he would suddenly emerge and appear before me as before. It sometimes happened that I was too incensed to ask him what he wanted, but I would simply raise my head sharply and imperiously, and then I too would stare back at him. And so we would stare at each other, for about two minutes; finally, slowly and pompously, he would turn round and retire for another two hours.

If this still failed to make me see reason and I continued to be rebellious, he would suddenly start sighing as he looked at me, drawing long, deep sighs as if by them alone he were gauging the whole depth of my moral decline, and needless to say this always ended in his complete victory over me: I would rage and scream, but I would still be compelled to do whatever had to be done.

On this occasion the usual manoeuvre of 'withering looks' had barely begun when I immediately lost my temper and flew at him in a fit of fury: I was exasperated enough as it was.

'Stop!' I shouted in a wild frenzy when, slowly and silently, one hand behind his back, he turned round to retire to his room. 'Stop! Come back, come back, I'm talking to you!' And I must have bellowed so unnaturally that he turned back and started eyeing me with some amazement. However, he still wouldn't say a word and it was this that really made me see red.

'How dare you come in here without permission and look at me like that! Answer me!'

But after calmly surveying me for half a minute he again started turning away.

'Stop!' I roared, running over to him. 'Don't move! That's it! Now answer me: why have you come in here to gawk at me like that?'

'If you have any orders for me right now it's my duty to carry them out,' he replied after another silence, with his soft, measured lisp, raising his eyebrows and calmly shifting his head from one shoulder to the other – all this with the most maddening composure.

'No, it's not that, that's not what I'm asking you about, you torturer!' I cried, shaking with anger. 'I'll tell you myself, you torturer, why you came here. You see that I'm not paying you your wages and since you're too proud to come and ask for them that's why you come in here to punish me with those inane stares of yours, to torment me. You do not sus-pe-ect for one moment, you torturer, how stupid it is, how stupid, stupid, stupid, stupid!'

He was again about to turn away without speaking, but I grabbed him.

'Listen!' I shouted. 'Here's the money. Look – look! Here it is (I took it out of the table drawer), all seven roubles, but you won't receive them, you won't re-ce-ive them until you come to me cap in hand, admitting your guilt and begging forgiveness. Do you hear me?!'

'But that can never be!' he replied with a kind of unnatural self-assurance.

'Oh yes it can!' I shouted. 'I give you my word of honour it can!'

'But I've no reason to ask for forgiveness,' he continued as if he simply hadn't noticed my shouts, 'because you called me "torturer" and for that I could always go along to the police station and put in a complaint.'

'Go then! Go and complain!' I roared. 'Go right away, this minute, this second! But you're a torturer all the same. Torturer, torturer!' But he merely glanced at me, then wheeled round, turned a deaf ear to my adjurations and sailed off to his quarters without once looking back.

'If it weren't for Liza none of this would have happened,' I said to myself. And then, after standing still for a moment, I followed him to his room behind the screen, solemnly and with dignity, but with my heart beating slowly and violently.

'Apollon!' I said with calm deliberation, although I was choking with anger. 'Go now, without a moment's delay and fetch the local police inspector.'

Meanwhile he had seated himself at his table, donned his spectacles and applied himself to some sewing. But on hearing my command, he suddenly snorted with laughter.

'Now, go this minute – go, or you can't imagine what will happen!'

'You must be truly out of your mind,' he remarked without even looking up, with that same slow lisp and continuing to thread his needle. 'Whoever heard of someone going to report himself to the police? And as for scaring me, you're wasting your energy, because nothing will come of it.'

'Go!!' I screeched, grabbing him by the collar. I felt I was on the verge of hitting him.

But I hadn't heard the entrance hall door quietly and slowly open all of a sudden and a figure entered and stopped to stare at us in bewilderment. I took one look, was stricken with shame and rushed off to my room. There, clutching my hair with both hands, I leant my head against the wall and froze in that position.

Two minutes later I heard Apollon's slow footsteps.

'There's a certain *person* asking for you,' he said, giving me a particularly severe look and then he stood aside to make way for Liza. He didn't want to leave and kept staring at us sarcastically.

'Get out! Get out!' I ordered, losing all self-control.

At that moment my clock exerted itself, wheezed and struck seven.

IX

And boldly and freely
Enter my house, mistress of all . . .
From the same poem

I stood before her, crushed, disgraced, sickeningly embarrassed – and, I think, smiling and making a concerted effort to wrap the skirts of my ragged old quilted dressing-gown around me – well, in every respect, exactly as I imagined shortly before, when my spirits were so low. After hovering over us for about two minutes Apollon went out, but I didn't feel any easier. And the worst of it was that she too suddenly became embarrassed, to a degree I had never even expected. Needless to say, it was from looking at me.

'Sit down,' I said mechanically, bringing a chair up to the table for her. She sat down immediately, obediently, all eyes, and she was evidently expecting something from me there and then. The naivety of this expectancy drove me into a frenzy but I controlled myself.

At this point I should have pretended not to notice anything, as if everything were normal, but she . . . And I vaguely sensed that she would make me pay dearly *for all this*.

'You've caught me in a strange situation, Liza,' I began, stammering and fully aware that this was exactly the wrong way to begin. 'No, no, don't think badly of it!' I cried, seeing that she had suddenly blushed, 'I'm not ashamed of my poverty . . . On the contrary, I look upon it with pride. I'm poor but honourable . . . It's possible to be poor and honourable . . .' I muttered. 'However . . . would you like some tea?'

'No.' she began.

'Wait a moment!'

I leapt up and dashed off to get Apollon. I had to disappear somewhere.

'Apollon,' I whispered in a feverish patter, tossing him the seven roubles that had been in my fist the whole time. 'Here's your wages. You see, I'm paying you, but in return you must save me. Now run down to the pub right away and bring some tea and ten dry biscuits. If you refuse you'll make me the unhappiest of mortals. You don't know what kind of woman she is . . . That's the whole point! Perhaps you're thinking things . . . But you don't know what kind of woman she is . . . !'

Apollon, who had already settled down to his work and had donned his spectacles again, without putting down his needle, at first squinted at the money in silence; then, ignoring me completely and still without a word, carried on fiddling with the thread, still trying to get it through the eye of the needle. I waited for about three minutes, standing before him with my arms folded à la Napoléon. My temples were damp with sweat and I sensed my face was pale. But, thank God, just looking at me must have made him feel sorry. Having finished with his thread, he slowly got up, slowly moved his chair back, slowly took off his spectacles, slowly counted the money and finally left the room after asking me over his shoulder whether he should fetch two full teas. As I went back to Liza the thought occurred to me of simply running away, just as I was, in my old dressing-gown, wherever my feet carried me – and come what may.

I sat down again. Liza looked at me anxiously. For a few minutes neither of us spoke.

'I'll kill him!' I suddenly shrieked, banging my fist so violently on the table that the ink splashed out of the inkwell.

'Ah, what are you saying?' she cried, shuddering.

'I'll kill him, I'll kill him!' I shouted, again banging on the table in a terrible rage, at the same time terribly aware how stupid it was to get into such a rage . . .

'You don't know how he tortures me, Liza. He's my executioner . . . Now he's gone out for some biscuits, he . . .'

And suddenly I burst into tears. It was a genuine attack of nerves. How ashamed I felt in between my fits of sobbing, but I was powerless to restrain them. She took fright.

'What's the matter with you? What's wrong?' she cried, fussing around me.

'Water, give me some water . . . it's over there,' I muttered feebly, aware, however, that I could very well manage without water and stop those feeble mutterings. But I was play-acting, as they say, to save face, although the nervous attack was real enough.

She gave me some water and looked at me with a lost expression. At that moment Apollon brought in the tea. This ordinary, prosaic tea suddenly struck me as so inappropriate and miserable after all that had happened that I blushed. Liza even glanced at Apollon in fright. He went out without so much as looking at us.

'Liza, do you despise me?' I asked, staring intently at her and trembling with impatience to discover what she was thinking.

She became flustered and was at a loss for a reply.

'Drink your tea!' I said angrily. I was furious with myself, but of course I had to make her suffer for it. Suddenly terrible anger towards her boiled up within me. I really think I could have killed her. To take revenge on her I vowed to myself not to say one word to her the whole time. 'She's to blame for everything,' I thought.

Our silence had already lasted about five minutes. The tea stood on the table but we didn't make any attempt to touch it. I had reached the point where I deliberately refused to begin first in order to make things even harder for her; for her to begin would have been awkward.

Several times she glanced at me in sad bewilderment. I remained stubbornly silent. Of course, the principal sufferer was myself, since I fully recognized the sickening meanness of my stupid anger and at the same time in no way could I restrain myself.

'I want ... to get away from that place ... altogether ...' she began in an attempt to break the silence somehow. But poor girl! That was precisely *not* the thing to bring up at a moment that was stupid enough already – and particularly to a stupid man like myself. My heart even ached with pity at her awkwardness and needless honesty. But something very nasty immediately stifled all pity within me. Indeed, it even spurred me on all the more. To hell with the whole world! Another five minutes went by.

'I'm not disturbing you, am I?' she began timidly and barely audibly, starting to get up.

But as soon as I saw this first flash of wounded dignity I simply shook with rage and immediately erupted.

'Why have you come here? Please tell me that,' I began, choking with anger and without considering even the logical sequence of my words. I wanted to get it all out at once, in one salvo, and I couldn't even be bothered about where to begin.

'Why did you come? Answer me! Answer me!' I shouted, beside myself. 'I'll tell you why you came, my dear woman. You came because I spoke *words of sympathy* to you the other night. Well, now you've gone soft and want to hear 'words of sympathy' again. Well, let me tell you that I was laughing at you then. And I'm laughing at you now. Why are you trembling? Yes, I was laughing! I'd been insulted before at a dinner by that same crowd who arrived before me. I came to your place intending to give one of them – an officer – a good thrashing. I wasn't successful, as he'd already left. So, I needed to vent my anger on someone because of that insult, to get my own back, and then you turned up, so I vented my anger on you and had a good laugh about it. I'd been humiliated, so I too wanted to humiliate someone. I'd been treated like a door-mat, so I wanted to show my power . . . That's how it was, but you were thinking that I'd come specially to rescue you, weren't you? Isn't that what you were thinking? Isn't it?'

I knew that she was perhaps getting confused and wouldn't grasp every detail; but I also knew that she understood the essence of what I was saying perfectly. And so she did. She turned white as a sheet, tried to speak, but her lips became painfully distorted and she slumped back into her chair as if felled by an axe. And all the time after this she listened to me open-mouthed, wide-eyed, trembling with terrible fear. The cynicism, the cynicism of my words had crushed her . . .

'To save you!' I continued, leaping from my chair and running up and down the room in front of her, 'to save you from what? Well, perhaps I'm worse than you. Why didn't you fling it all back in my mug when I was preaching to you? You asked: 'Why did you come here? To teach us morality?' It was power, power that I wanted then and I wanted some sport, I needed your tears, your humiliation, your hysterics – that's what I needed then! But I myself couldn't go through with it because I'm trash, I panicked and the devil knows why I was stupid enough to give you my address. Later, even before I got home, I was cursing you to high heaven, because of that address. I really did hate you because I'd lied to you then. Because I only wanted to have a little game with words, to fill my head with dreams – but do you know what I really wanted? For you to vanish into thin air, that's what! I need peace and quiet. And in order not to be disturbed I'd sell the whole world right now for a copeck. Should the world vanish or should I go without my tea? I'm telling you, the whole world can vanish as long as I always have my tea to drink. Did you know that or not? What I do know is that I'm a scoundrel, a cad, an egotist, a loafer. Oh yes, for the past three days I've been shaking for fear that you might come. And do you know what particularly worried me during those three days? That I'd made myself out to be such a great hero before you then – and that suddenly you'd find me here in this shabby old dressing-gown, destitute and loathsome. I told you just now that I wasn't ashamed of my poverty. Well, please understand that I *am* ashamed, ashamed of it more than anything. I fear it more than anything, more than if I'd stolen something, because I'm so vain – it's as if I've been flayed alive and the very air causes me pain. Surely you must realize even now that I'll never forgive you for having caught me in this wretched old dressing-gown, just when I was hurling myself like a vicious little cur at Apollon. The saviour, the former hero, flying like a mangy, shaggy mongrel at his servant – and he just laughs at him! And as for those tears which I couldn't hold back just before, like some old crone who's been put to shame – I shall never forgive you those! Nor will I ever forgive *you* for what I'm confessing to you now! Oh yes, you – you alone must answer for everything, now that you've turned up, because I'm a cad, the vilest, most ridiculous, pettiest, stupidest, most jealous of all the worms on earth, not one jot better than me but who, the devil knows why, are never embarrassed. But all my life I'll be insulted by any little nit because that's what my character's like! And what's it to do with me if you don't understand a word of all this! And why should it concern me whether you perish in that place or not? And do you realize that now, having said all this, how I shall hate you for having been here and listened to me? After all, it's only once in a lifetime that a man speaks his mind like this and then only if he's hysterical! What more do you want? Why are you still hanging around after all this, tormenting me by not leaving?'

But then something very odd happened.

I was so used to thinking and imagining things as they happened in books and picturing everything in the world as I myself had previously created it in my dreams, that at first I couldn't understand that strange event. What happened was this: Liza, whom I had so humiliated and crushed, understood a lot more than I imagined. She understood from all this what a woman will always understand first and foremost if she loves sincerely, namely, that I myself was unhappy.

At first the terrified and wronged expression on her face turned into sorrowful amazement. But when I began to call myself a cad and a rotter and my tears started flowing (I had delivered all of my tirade in tears) her whole face was distorted by some kind of convulsion. She wanted to get up, to stop me; but when I had finished it wasn't to my cries of 'Why are you here, why don't you leave?' that she paid attention, but to the fact that it must have been extremely hard for me to say all I had said. And she was so dispirited, poor thing; she considered herself infinitely beneath me. But why should she feel animosity and take offence? Suddenly, on some kind of irresistible impulse, she leapt from her chair and then, her whole body straining towards me – timidly, though, and without daring to move from her seat – she held out her arms to me . . . At this point my heart too turned over. Then she suddenly rushed towards me, threw her arms around my neck and burst into tears. I couldn't hold myself back either and sobbed as I had never sobbed before . . .

'They won't let me . . . I can't be . . . kind!' I barely managed to say and then I reached the sofa, fell face downwards on it and sobbed really hysterically for a quarter of an hour. She pressed herself against me, embraced me and seemed to freeze in that embrace.

All the same, the point was that my hysterics could not last for ever. And now (I'm writing the whole sickening truth), as I lay face down, pressing hard against the sofa, my face buried in my cheap leather cushion, I began gradually, as if from a distance, involuntarily but irrepressibly, to feel that it would be awkward if I were to raise my head now and look Liza straight in the eye. What was I ashamed of? I don't know, but I was ashamed. And the thought also entered my overwrought brain that our roles had now been completely reversed, that she was the heroine and that I was just such a humiliated and crushed creature as she had appeared to me that night – four days before . . . And all this occurred to me just when I was lying face down on the sofa!

Good God! Could I have envied her even then?

I don't know, to this day I still cannot decide, but then I was of course even less able to understand it than I am now. Without power and tyranny over someone I cannot survive. But . . . but reasoning won't solve anything, so there's no point in reasoning.

However, I pulled myself together and raised my head slightly – I had to raise it some time or other . . . And then, I am convinced of it to this day, it was precisely because I was ashamed of looking at her that another feeling was suddenly kindled in my heart and flared up . . . a feeling of mastery and possession. My eyes gleamed with passion and I squeezed her hand hard. How I hated her and how powerfully I was drawn to her at that moment! One feeling reinforced the other. This was almost tantamount to revenge . . . ! At first her face expressed what seemed to be perplexity, perhaps even fear, but only for a fleeting instant. Rapturously and fervently she embraced me.

X

A quarter of an hour later I was rushing up and down the room in frantic impatience, constantly going over to the screens and peeping at Liza through the narrow gap between them. She was sitting on the floor, leaning her head on the bed and she must have been crying. But she was not leaving and it was this that irritated me. This time she knew everything. I had insulted her definitively, but there's no point in telling that story. She had guessed that my fit of passion was indeed revenge, a fresh humiliation for her, and that to my former, almost aimless hatred there was now added a *personal*, *jealous* hatred of her . . . However, I'm not claiming that she exactly understood all of this. On the other hand, she understood well enough that I was a loathsome person and, most important, incapable of loving her.

I know that people will tell me that it's incredible – incredible to be as spiteful and stupid as I am. And perhaps they will add that it was incredible not to fall in love with her, or at least appreciate her love. But why incredible? Firstly, I was incapable of falling in love because, I repeat, to me love meant tyrannizing and being morally superior. All my life I've been unable even to imagine any other kind of love and I've reached the point where I sometimes think that love consists in the right, voluntarily given by the loved one, to be tyrannized. Even in my underground dreams I couldn't conceive of love as other than a struggle that I invariably embarked upon with hatred and finished with moral subjugation, after which I couldn't imagine what to do with the vanquished victim. And in fact the incredible thing here is that I had already managed to become so morally corrupt and had grown so accustomed to 'real life' that only just now had I thought of reproaching her and putting her to shame for coming to hear my 'words of sympathy'. And I didn't guess that she hadn't come to hear words of sympathy at all, but to love me, since for women love comprises their total resurrection, their total salvation from any kind of ruin, their total regeneration and cannot manifest itself in any other kind of way. However, I no longer hated her so much as I scurried around the room, peeping through the gap between the screens. I only felt it intolerably oppressive with her being there. I wanted her to disappear. I longed for 'peace', I wanted to be left alone in my underground. I had become so unused to 'real life' that it crushed me until I even found it hard to breathe.

But a few more minutes passed and still she didn't get up, as if she were in a trance. I was shameless enough to knock gently on the screen to remind her . . . Suddenly she roused herself, leapt from her place and hurriedly started looking for her shawl, her hat, her fur coat, as if escaping from me somewhere. Two minutes later she slowly came out from behind the screens and gave me a pained look. I produced a spiteful smile, that was forced however, *for the sake of decency*, and turned away from her stare.

'Goodbye,' she said, heading towards the door.

I suddenly ran after her, grabbed her hand, unclasped it, put something into it and then clasped it again. Then I immediately turned away and rushed as fast as I could to the far corner so that at least I wouldn't see . . .

At that moment I wanted to tell a lie, to write that I had done it unintentionally, without thinking, while beside myself, out of stupidity. But I don't want to lie and therefore I say straight out that I unclasped her hand and put something into it . . . out of spite. The idea had occurred to me when I was running up and down the room while she was sitting behind the screens. But what I can say for certain is this: although I committed this act of cruelty deliberately, it came not from the heart but from my wicked head. This cruelty was so artificial, so cerebral, so deliberately contrived, so *bookish*, that I myself couldn't sustain it even for a minute – first I dashed into the corner in order not to see, then, ashamed and desperate, I rushed after Liza. I opened the hall door and listened hard.

'Liza! Liza!' I called down the stairs, timidly though, in an undertone . . .

There was no answer and I thought I could hear her footsteps on the lower stairs.

'Liza!' I shouted, louder this time.

No reply. But at that moment I could hear the heavy glazed street door creak open and slam shut. The noise carried up the staircase.

She had gone. Hesitantly, I returned to my room. I felt utterly miserable.

I stopped at the table near the chair where she had been sitting and gazed vacantly in front of me. About a minute passed, then suddenly I trembled all over: right before me on the table I saw . . . in brief, I saw a crumpled, blue five-rouble note, the very one that I had thrust into her hand a moment before. It was the *same one*: it couldn't have been any other, as there was no other in the house. She must have managed to fling it on the table just as I was dashing to the opposite corner.

What then? I might have expected her to do that. Might have expected? No. I was such a egotist and in actual fact had so little respect for others that I couldn't imagine that she would do such a thing. This was more than I could bear. A moment later I rushed like a madman to get dressed, throwing on whatever I could in my frantic hurry and then rushing headlong after her. She hadn't gone more than a couple of hundred yards when I ran out into the street.

It was quiet and the snow was coming down in large flakes, falling almost perpendicularly and spreading a soft white blanket over the pavement and the deserted street. There were no passers-by, not a sound could be heard. The street lamps glimmered mournfully and uselessly. I ran about two hundred paces to the crossroads and stopped.

'Where had she gone? And why am I running after her? Why? To go down on my knees, to break into repentant sobs, to kiss her feet, to beg her forgiveness? That was just what I wanted. My heart was being torn to shreds and never, never shall I recall that moment with indifference. But why – why?' I thought. 'Surely I'd hate her, perhaps tomorrow, precisely because I kissed her feet today? Could I really have made her happy? Surely I'd recognized my own true worth again today, for the hundredth time? Surely I'd torment the life out of her!'

I stood in the snow, peering into the dull haze and thought about it.

'And isn't it better, wouldn't it be better,' I daydreamed later at home, trying to deaden the sharp pain in my heart with my fantasies, wouldn't it be better if she took that insult to her pride away with her for ever? After all, an insult is purification; it is the most caustic and painful form of consciousness! Tomorrow I would have defiled her soul and wearied her heart by my presence. But now that insult will never die within her and however vile the filth that is in store for her, that insult will elevate and purify her . . . through hatred . . . hm . . . and perhaps through forgiveness. However, will all this make life any the easier for her? And in fact I'll now pose one idle question: which is better – cheap happiness or exalted suffering? Tell me, which is better?

All this dimly appeared to me as I sat at home that evening, half-dead with spiritual pain. I have never endured such suffering and repentance. But really, could there ever have been even the slightest doubt, when I ran out of the flat, that I would turn back halfway and go home? Never again did I meet Liza, nor did I hear what became of her. I will add that for a long time I remained pleased with my *windy rhetoric* about the usefulness of insults and hatred – despite the fact that I myself became almost ill with anguish at the time.

And even now, after so many years, all this comes back as a *nasty* memory. Many things are now nasty memories, but . . . shouldn't I really end the 'Notes' here? It seems that writing them in the first place was a mistake. At least, I felt ashamed the whole time I was writing this *tale*. That means it is not literature, but corrective punishment. For example, telling a long story about how I missed out on life in my corner through moral decay, through lack of human contact, through losing the habit of living and through my narcissistic, underground spite – God, that's of no interest! A novel needs a hero but here I've *deliberately* gathered together all the features of an anti-hero and the main thing is, all this will produce a most unpleasant impression, since we have all lost touch with real life, we are all cripples, each one of us to a greater or lesser degree. We have even become so unaccustomed to living that we sometimes feel a kind of loathing for 'real life' and that's why we cannot bear to be reminded of it. You see, we have reached the point where we look upon real life almost as a burden, almost as servitude, and we are all agreed among ourselves that it's better to live according to books. And what are all of us sometimes rummaging around for, why are we so capricious, what is it we are begging for? We ourselves don't know. It would be even worse for us if our capricious requests were granted. Well, just try, give us more independence, for intance, loosen the bonds of any one of us, broaden our field of activity, relax surveillance and we . . . yes, I assure you we should all immediately be begging for that surveillance to be reimposed. I know that you will perhaps be angry with me because of this, you'll stamp your feet and say: 'You are speaking of yourself alone and your underground misery, so don't you dare say *all of us*.' But excuse me, gentlemen, I'm not trying to justify myself by this *all of usness*. Strictly speaking, as far as I'm concerned, I've merely carried to extremes in my life things that you've never had the courage even to take halfway and what's more you've interpreted your cowardice as common sense and found comfort in deceiving yourselves. So perhaps I'll prove to be 'more alive' than you. And just take a closer look. After all, we don't even know where this 'living' life is lived these days, what it is or what its name is. Leave us to our own devices, without our books, and we'll immediately get into a muddle and lose our way – we shan't know what side to take, where to place our allegiance, what to love and what to hate, what to respect and what to despise. We even find it a burden being human beings – human beings with our *own* real flesh and blood; we are ashamed of it, consider it a disgrace and are forever striving to become some kind of imaginary generalized human beings. We are stillborn and we have long ceased to be begotten of living fathers – and this we find increasingly pleasing. We are acquiring a taste for it. Soon we'll devise a way of being somehow born from an idea. But that's enough: I don't want to write any more from 'The Underground . . .'

On the other hand, the 'Notes' of this purveyor of paradoxes do not end here. He couldn't help continuing with them. But we also feel that here we might call a halt.

Notes

1. *collegiate assessor*: Eighth grade in Table of Ranks, equivalent to army major.
2. *'sublime and beautiful'*: Term used by, among others, Edmund Burke. The Underground Man uses this Romantic term frequently with great irony.
3. *l'homme de la nature et de la vérité*: This phrase appears differently in Rousseau's *Confessions* (1782–9), and it seems Dostoyevsky is deliberately and sarcastically misquoting *Première Partie*, Livre Premier: 'Je forme une entreprise qui n'eut jamais d'exemple, et dont l'exécution n'aura point d'imitateur. Je veux montrer à mes semblables un homme dans toute la vérité de la nature, et cet homme, ce sera moi.' ('I am undertaking something which has never had a precedent and whose execution will have no imitator. I wish to portray to my fellows a man in the whole truth of nature – and that man will be me.')

   Dostoyevsky here follows Heine's total scepticism concerning the possibility of true autobiography. Affirming that no one up to then had succeeded in writing a true autobiography, Heine states in Part 10 of volume two of the French edition of *De l'Allemagne*, in his *Confessions* (1853–4): '. . . ni le Genevois Jean-Jacques Rousseau; surtout ce dernier qui, tout en s'appellant l'homme de la vérité et de la nature, n'était au fond pas moins mensonger et dénaturé que les autres.' ('. . . neither the Genevan Jean-Jacques Rousseau; above all the latter who, calling himself a man of nature and truth, was basically no less mendacious and perverted than others').
4. *Once it is proven to you, for example, that you're descended from the apes . . .*: Interest in the question of man's origin had particularly sharpened at the beginning of 1864 with the appearance in translation, in St Petersburg, of T. H. Huxley's *Evidence as to Man's Place in Nature* (1863).

5. *... despite all the Wagenheims in the world ...*: According to a directory, in the mid-1860s there were no fewer than eight dentists of this name in St Petersburg; signboards advertising their services were to be seen all over the city.
6. *... like a person "divorced from the soil and his native roots" ...*: This phrase occurs frequently in articles appearing in Dostoyevsky's journals of the early 1860s – *Time* and *Epoch*.
7. *... the artist Ge*: Dostoyevsky is here attacking an article by the novelist and publicist M. E. Saltykov-Shchedrin praising a painting by N. N. Ge (1831–94), *The Last Supper*, shown at the Academy of Arts autumn exhibition of 1863. This painting aroused conflicting criticisms and Dostoyevsky later reproached Ge for deliberately mixing the historical with the contemporary, which resulted in falsehood (*Diary of a Writer*, 1873, IX). 'For your satisfaction' was an article of Saltykov-Shchedrin's, printed in *The Contemporary*, 1863.
8. *... affirming with Buckle ...*: H. T. Buckle (1821–62), in his *History of Civilisation in England* (1863), had expounded the idea that the development of civilization leads to the cessation of war between nations.
9. *There's your Napoleon ... the present-day one*: Napoleon I and Napoleon III are mentioned in view of the great number of wars waged by France during their reigns.
10. *There's your North America ...*: Reference to the American Civil War (1861–5).
11. *... there's your grotesque Schleswig-Holstein*: By 'grotesque' Dostoyevsky is probably referring to the immensely complicated history of Schleswig-Holstein. Briefly, the duchies of Schleswig and Holstein became the personal possessions of the King of Denmark in 1460, with a largely German population. Holstein was included in the German Confederation (1815). In 1848 Prussia intervened to stop a Danish attempt to annex the duchies and, together with Austria, forced Denmark to give them up (1864), Austria taking Holstein and Prussia Schleswig.
12. *Attila*: King of the Huns (c. 406–53) who overran much of the Byzantine and Western Roman Empires. He came to be called the 'Scourge of God'.
13. *Stenka Razin*: Don Cossack (?–1671) who led a peasant revolt in 1670, causing widespread devastation and massacring landowners. There is a portrait of him in Turgenev's story 'Phantoms', published together with *Notes from Underground* in the same issue of *Epoch*.

14. *Cleopatra*: Queen of Egypt (69–30 BC). Her name was mentioned frequently in the Russian press in 1861, in connection with the reading at a literary evening in Perm of her monologue in Pushkin's 'Egyptian Nights' (1835), by Madame Tolmachev, a civil servant's wife. This reading is mentioned with great relish by the libertine Svidrigaylov in *Crime and Punishment*.
15. *Then the Crystal Palace will be erected*: The Crystal Palace is referred to in 'The Fourth Dream of Vera Pavlovna' in N. G. Chernyshevsky's utopian novel *What is to be Done?* (1863), the main target of Dostoyevsky's polemic in *Notes from Underground*. Chernyshevsky describes a cast-iron crystal palace as presented by Charles Fourier in his *Theory of Universal Unity* (1841); in this crystal palace members of a social commune or phalanstery live in complete harmony. Here the model (for the palace) was the Crystal Palace built in 1851 for the Great Exhibition in London.
16. *Colossus of Rhodes*: Bronze statue of Helios 31 metres high, cast in 280 BC and one of the Seven Wonders of the World.
17. *Mr Anayevsky*: A. E. Anayevsky (1788–1866), author of literary articles, the object of constant ridicule in journals of the 1840s–60s. In his brochure 'Enchiridion for the Curious' he writes: 'The Colossus of Rhodes was erected, some writers affirm by Semiramis, others claim it was not erected by human hands, but by Nature.'
18. *aux animaux domestiques*: To domestic animals.
19. *. . . Heine claims . . . lie about himself*: In *De l'Allemagne*, volume two in his *Confessions* (1853–4), Heine wrote: 'To execute one's own self-portrait would not only be an awkward undertaking but simply impossible . . . for all one's desire to be sincere, not one man can tell the truth about himself.' In the same book he affirms that in his *Confessions* Rousseau 'makes false confessions to hide his true actions behind them' (see also note 3).
20. *. . . apropos of the wet snow*: The memoirist P. V. Annenkov in his article 'Notes on Russian Literature' observed that 'fine drizzle and wet snow are indispensable elements of the St Petersburg cityscape with writers of the Natural School and their imitators'.
21. *When from error's murky ways . . .*: From the poem by the civic poet N. A. Nekrasov (1845). This poem was one of the first where Nekrasov treats a fallen woman with great compassion and it had been mentioned ironically in *The Village of Stepanchikovo* (1859).

With the three etceteras that unceremoniously close the quotation, Dostoyevsky is treating with much sarcasm the redeemed prostitute theme originating in French Social Romantic novelists such as Eugène Sue, Victor Hugo and George Sand, and which appears in Chernyshevsky's *What is to be Done?*, which he is polemicizing in *Notes from Underground*. There is a strong resemblance between the episode in *What is to be Done?* where a hero saves a fallen woman who eventually dies of tuberculosis, and that in the second part of *Notes from Underground*.

22. *Kostanzhoglos and Uncle Pyotr Ivanoviches*: Kostanzhoglo, a model landowner portrayed by Gogol in Part Two of *Dead Souls* (1843–6); Pyotr Ivanovich (Aduyev): the uncle in Goncharov's *An Ordinary Story* (1847), the epitome of hard-headed practicality.
23. *... because he thinks he's the 'King of Spain'*: Poprishchin in Gogol's *Diary of a Madman* (1835) is under the illusion he's King of Spain.
24. *... like Gogol's Lieutenant Pirogov*: In *Nevsky Prospekt* (1835) Pirogov, after being flogged by the tinsmith Schiller for flirting with his wife, wishes to put in a written complaint to the authorities.
25. *Fatherland Notes*: (1839–84) Founded by A. Krayevsky and considered the leading journal of the Westernizers. Works by Lermontov, Belinsky, Turgenev, Herzen and Nekrasov were published in it.
26. *Nevsky Prospekt*: St Petersburg's main thoroughfare, about two and a half miles long, the hub of the city's shopping and entertainment district. Gogol's description of it in his story of that name makes an interesting comparison with Dostoyevsky's.
27. *Gostiny Dvor*: Shopping arcade opening off Nevsky Prospekt. It is visited by Golyadkin on his mad shopping spree in *The Double* (1846).
28. *Manfredian*: After Manfred, eponymous hero of Byron's dramatic poem (1817), the personification of romantic despondency.
29. *... rout the reactionaries at Austerlitz*: The hero imagines himself as Napoleon, victor over the combined Russian and Austrian forces (1805). There is possibly a reflection here of a novel known to Dostoyevsky, E. Cabet's *Voyage en Icarie* (1840), where the philosopher-reformer of mankind also smashes the coalition of the 'retrograde' emperors at Austerlitz.
30. *... the Pope agrees to leave Rome for Brazil*: Refers to conflict between Napoleon I and Pope Pius VII – as a result of which

Napoleon was excommunicated – from 1809 to 1814, during which time the Pope was a virtual prisoner of Napoleon.

31. *... ball for the whole of Italy at the Villa Borghese*: Refers to celebration in 1806 of the foundation of the French Empire, arranged to coincide with the birthday of Napoleon. The Villa Borghese was established in Rome in the first half of the eighteenth century. At the time it belonged to Camillo Borghese, husband of Napoleon's sister Polina.
32. *Five Corners*: Place in St Petersburg at the junction of Zagorodny Prospekt, Chernyshev Alley, Razezzhaya Street and Troitskaya Street.
33. *Zverkov*: From *zver* (wild animal), a name that reflects its bearer's character. This may be compared with the name of Simonov's other guest, *Trudolyubov* (p. 57), from '*trud*' (toil) and '*lyubov*' (love), which suggests an industrious person.
34. *droit de seigneur*: Medieval feudal custom where the lord had the right to spend the wedding night with the bride of one of his vassals.
35. *Silvio*: From Pushkin's story *The Shot* (*Tales of Belkin*, 1830). After a wealthy count refuses to treat a duel seriously, Silvio retains the right to fire at the count at any time. Bursting in on the happily married count and his wife, however, he takes pity and wastes his shot.
36. *Masquerade*: Drama by Mikhail Lermontov, written in 1835–6, where the demonic villain Arbenin poisons his wife on suspicion of infidelity, only to go insane when he learns that she is innocent.
37. *the Haymarket*: Originally fodder and livestock were sold there in the 1730s. The surrounding area was inhabited by the poor and the whole neighbourhood was filled with brothels, gambling dens and low pubs. The dreadful squalor there is vividly evoked in *Crime and Punishment*.
38. *Volkovo Cemetery*: Volkovo Kladbishche, or Wolves' Graveyard, so called as the area was originally overrun with vicious wolves. Founded for the burial of the poor, the cemetery grew in size and became the last resting place of the famous, including Turgenev, Belinsky, Kropotkin, Witte and Blok.
39. *the Sadovaya, and near the Yusupov Gardens*: Sadovaya Street runs through the Haymarket as far as Nevsky Prospekt. The Yusupov Gardens lie just to the south of the Haymarket, off Sadovaya Street.
40. *And boldly and freely ...*: From the poem by Nekrasov that appears as epigraph to Part II of *Notes from Underground* (p. 38).

THE STORY OF PENGUIN CLASSICS

Before 1946... 'Classics' are mainly the domain of academics and students; readable editions for everyone else are almost unheard of. This all changes when a little-known classicist, E. V. Rieu, presents Penguin founder Allen Lane with the translation of Homer's *Odyssey* that he has been working on in his spare time.

1946 Penguin Classics debuts with *The Odyssey*, which promptly sells three million copies. Suddenly, classics are no longer for the privileged few.

1950s Rieu, now series editor, turn to professional writers for the best modern, readable translations, including Dorothy L. Sayers's *Inferno* and Robert Grave's unexpurgated *Twelve Caesars*.

1960s The Classics are given the distinctive black covers that have remained a constant throughout the life of the series. Rieu retires in 1964, hailing the Penguin Classics list as the 'greatest educative force of the twentieth century'.

1970s The list grows to encompass more history, philosophy, science, religion and politics.

1980s The Penguin American Library launches with titles such as *Uncle Tom's Cabin*, and joins forces with Penguin Classics to provide the most comprehensive library of world literature available from any paperback publisher.

1990s The launch of Penguin Audiobooks brings the classics to a listening audience for the first time, and in 1999 the worldwide launch of the Penguin Classics website extends their reach to the global online community.

The 21st Century Penguin Classics are completely redesigned for the first time in nearly twenty years. This world-famous series now consists of more than 1300 titles, making the widest range of the best books ever written available to millions – and constantly redefining what makes a 'classic'.

2010 Penguin Classics partners with (PRODUCT)RED™ to create (PENGUIN CLASSICS)RED from which 50% of profits go to the Global Fund to help eliminate AIDS in Africa. Now great literature can help save lives.

The Odyssey continues...